Loch Ness has a Secret

Paula Fulton

—

Published by Kinetic Digital Publishers
www.kineticdigitalpublishers.com
For permissions, inquiries, or other correspondence, please visit our website.

ISBN eBook: 979-8-90235-040-8
ISBN Paperback: 979-8-90235-035-4

LCCN: 2025927866

Dedication

This book is dedicated to the unwavering spirit of exploration and the boundless curiosity that drives us to unravel the mysteries of our world, both seen and unseen. It is a testament to those who dare to challenge conventional wisdom, to those who pursue the seemingly impossible with unwavering determination, and to those who find wonder in the unexpected.

It is dedicated to the countless individuals who have dedicated their lives to the pursuit of cryptozoology, a field often met with skepticism and ridicule, yet one that holds the potential to reshape our understanding of the natural world and our place within it. Their tireless efforts, meticulous research, and unwavering belief in the existence of the extraordinary inspire us all to look beyond the obvious and embrace the wonder of the unknown.

This book is also dedicated to the children who possess an innate sense of wonder and a boundless capacity for believing in magic and mystery. It is for those young minds who still hold onto the possibility of creatures beyond our comprehension, who see the extraordinary in the ordinary, and who dream of adventures that transcend the boundaries of reality. May their imaginations never cease to soar, and may they always hold onto the belief that the most extraordinary discoveries are waiting just around the corner, hidden in plain sight or submerged deep within the mysteries of our world.

It is dedicated to the enduring allure of the Loch Ness Monster, a symbol of mystery and wonder that has captivated the imaginations of people across generations. Nessie, whether a creature of myth or reality, serves as a powerful reminder of the countless secrets still held by our planet, secrets waiting to be unveiled by those brave enough to seek them out. This dedication is an acknowledgement of the enduring power of mystery and the boundless potential for discovery that lies within the unexplored corners of our world. Finally, this book is dedicated to everyone who has ever looked into the depths of Loch Ness, felt the chill of a Scottish mist, and dreamt of uncovering a truth that could change everything. For it is in those dreams that the greatest adventures begin.

TABLE OF CONTENTS

Chapter 1

The Nessie Obsession

The air hung thick with the scent of peat smoke and damp earth, a smell that would forever be intertwined in my memory with the image that seared itself onto my eight-year-old mind. It was a summer afternoon, the kind that paints the Scottish Highlands in a hazy, golden light. My grandfather, a man whose craggy face held the wisdom of a thousand hills and the stubbornness of a Highland cow, had taken me on our annual pilgrimage to Loch Ness. He'd promised me Nessie sightings, of course, a promise seasoned with the knowing twinkle in his eye that suggested a playful exaggeration rather than a genuine expectation.

We sat on the shore, the loch a shimmering, mirror reflecting the vast sky. The air was still, save for the occasional cry of a gull and the gentle lapping of water against the pebbled beach. My grandfather, his pipe clenched between his teeth, was regaling me with tales of the legendary creature, stories passed down through generations of MacDougalls. He spoke of ripples that defied explanation, of fleeting glimpses of something massive moving beneath the surface, of the disturbances in the sonar readings that baffled scientists. I listened, captivated, my imagination painting vivid pictures of a creature.

Suddenly, the stillness shattered. A disturbance rippled across the surface of the loch, not the gentle undulation of the wind, but a powerful surge that sent waves crashing against the shore. My grandfather's pipe fell from his lips, his eyes widening in a mixture of surprise and disbelief. Before either of us could utter a word, a massive, serpentine form broke the surface.

It was unlike anything I had ever seen. Not a log, not a boat, not a trick of the light. It was impossibly long, its dark, glistening skin reflecting the sunlight. Its movement was fluid, powerful, almost graceful, as it glided across the water. I remember the way the water parted before it, the way it seemed to displace the very air around it. Its head, partially submerged, was elongated, its form vaguely reptilian, with something that looked almost like a gentle crest along its back. It was an unforgettable sight, a moment frozen in time and memory.

The creature remained visible for what felt like an eternity, yet probably only lasted a few seconds. Then, with a powerful, almost effortless movement, it plunged back beneath the surface, leaving only a swirling vortex of water in its wake. Silence descended once more, heavier and more profound than before.

My grandfather, his face a mask of stunned silence, simply stared at the spot where the creature had disappeared. The pipe lay forgotten in the sand. For a moment, I thought he might not speak, the weight of what we'd just witnessed heavy in the air. Then, a slow, almost reverent smile spread across his weathered features. "Well," he finally whispered, his voice thick with emotion. "I guess she hasn't entirely forgotten how to put on a show."

But my experience that day was more than just a show. It wasn't the whimsical story of a fanciful creature. It was something profound, something that settled deep within my soul, igniting a spark of curiosity that would never be extinguished. I knew, even then, that I had witnessed something extraordinary, something that the skeptics and the doubters would never understand. They would dismiss it as a log, a boat, an illusion – anything but the magnificent creature I had seen with my own eyes.

Their skepticism only fueled my determination. While other children dreamt of becoming astronauts or firefighters, I dreamt of finding Nessie, of proving to the world that the legendary monster was real. I devoured books about cryptozoology, about the scientific pursuit of elusive creatures. I learned about the methods of evidence gathering, about the analysis of eyewitness accounts and physical evidence, about the crucial role of observation and deduction in uncovering the truth. I learned about the importance of differentiating between scientific investigation and pseudoscience, between meticulously collected data and fabricated claims. My childhood was filled with a mix of wonder and academic rigor, a pursuit that shaped my life in ways I could never have imagined.

My fascination with Loch Ness wasn't just about the monster itself; it was about the mystery, the enigma, the tantalizing possibility that something extraordinary could exist beyond the accepted boundaries of our understanding. It was a mystery embedded in the breathtaking beauty of the Scottish Highlands, a place of rugged mountains, mist-shrouded glens, and the ever-present allure of the loch itself. The very air seemed to hum with untold secrets, with whispers of ancient legends and forgotten lore. The wind seemed to carry echoes of stories, of those who lived and died by the shores of that mysterious lake, their lives entangled in the myth and the reality of Nessie.

That summer afternoon beside Loch Ness wasn't just a sighting; it was a call. A call to adventure, to discovery, to the pursuit of knowledge that transcended the mundane. It was a call that would shape the trajectory of my life, leading me down a path far more challenging, far more rewarding, and far more extraordinary than I could have ever imagined. It was a journey that started with a child's awe and would end with a scientist's relentless pursuit of the truth, a truth that lay hidden beneath the murky depths of Loch Ness and beyond, a truth entangled with hidden caves, strange lights in the night sky, and the unsettling possibility that time itself might not be as linear as we once believed.

The years that followed were a blur of relentless study and intellectual exploration. I devoured every textbook, every scientific paper, every historical account I could lay my hands on. I learned about the geological formations around Loch Ness, the history of the region, the ancient myths and legends surrounding the loch. I learned to analyze sonar data, to interpret blurry photographs, to identify patterns in seemingly random events. I honed my skills in observation, deduction, and critical thinking, skills that would prove invaluable in my future investigations.

My path wasn't easy. The field of cryptozoology is often viewed with skepticism, even ridicule. Many dismissed it as a pseudoscience, a field devoid of rigorous scientific method. But I persisted, driven by an unwavering belief in the power of observation, evidence, and careful analysis. I spent years poring over historical accounts, studying the physical properties of Loch Ness, and seeking explanations for the many anomalous events reported over the centuries. My doctoral thesis focused on the statistical analysis of unexplained disturbances in the loch, employing cutting-edge technology to examine the data with a new perspective. The project required tireless effort, long nights spent hunched over computer screens, sifting through data and analyzing results, seeking a pattern, a connection, a clue. The academic world, while occasionally frustrating in its skepticism, provided me with the tools and knowledge to navigate the complexities of the mystery.

I also encountered my share of doubters. Professors who questioned the validity of my research, colleagues who dismissed my theories as fanciful, friends who thought I was chasing an impossible dream. But their doubts only made me stronger, more determined to prove them wrong. I knew in my heart that something extraordinary existed within the depths of Loch Ness, something that the narrow confines of conventional science couldn't fully explain. That something extraordinary had shown itself to me as a child, and I was determined to unveil its secrets. The skepticism only deepened my resolve and sharpened my focus; every doubt fueled my quest for evidence and fueled my passion. The years of study and the challenges

I faced only increased my determination to find the answers I sought.

The pursuit of a doctorate in cryptozoology was not merely an academic exercise; it was a personal pilgrimage, a dedicated journey to understand and explain the extraordinary event I witnessed as a child. Each class, each research project, each late-night study session brought me closer to unlocking the mysteries that the skeptics had dismissed as fiction. It was a constant challenge to reconcile the scientific rigor with my deep-seated belief in the extraordinary. It was this very tension that fueled my determination, pushing me to explore the intersection of science, mystery, and the unknown. And it was this very combination of rigorous analysis and passionate belief that would ultimately lead me on the most extraordinary adventure of my life.

The hallowed halls of Edinburgh University held a different kind of magic than the misty shores of Loch Ness. Instead of the whispering reeds and the lapping water, there were hushed whispers of intellectual debate and the rustling of pages filled with complex equations and scientific jargon. My doctoral studies were a far cry from the idyllic childhood summers spent by the loch, but the unwavering focus remained the same: the Loch Ness Monster.

My initial proposal was met with raised eyebrows. Cryptozoology, even within the relatively open-minded environment of the university's zoology department, was considered by many to be on the fringes of acceptable academic inquiry. Some professors politely suggested alternative research topics, hinting at the lack of concrete evidence and the inherent difficulties of studying a creature whose very existence was questioned. But I persisted, presenting a meticulously crafted research proposal, outlining a statistical analysis of unexplained sonar anomalies and underwater disturbances reported in Loch Ness over the past century. My passion, the unwavering conviction born from my childhood experience, burned brighter than their skepticism.

The years that followed were a whirlwind of research. I spent countless hours in the university's archives, poring over decades worth of sonar data, eyewitness accounts, and blurry photographs. I learned to sift through the noise, to separate the credible reports from the fabrications, the genuine anomalies from the mundane explanations. I used advanced statistical modeling techniques to identify patterns in the data, searching for correlations, for evidence that pointed beyond chance occurrences. My days were filled with the hum of computers, the click-clack of keyboards, and the satisfying sense of progress as I uncovered new insights and refined my methodology.

The technical challenges were immense. The data sets were vast and inconsistent, spanning different technologies and methodologies over many years. I had to develop custom algorithms to process the raw data, accounting for variables such as weather patterns, water currents, and the movement of boats. My nights were often filled with troubleshooting code, battling cryptic error messages, and refining my analyses to ensure accuracy and eliminate bias. There were moments of frustration, of self-doubt, when the sheer volume of data and the complexity of the analysis seemed insurmountable. But my childhood experience, the memory of that magnificent creature, fueled my perseverance.

Beyond the technical hurdles, there was the constant battle against preconceived notions. My research faced scrutiny from academics who viewed cryptozoology with suspicion, dismissing it as a pseudoscience. Conferences were a mixed bag; some attendees engaged with my research intellectually, others responded with dismissive smirks and pointed questions designed to undermine my findings. The intellectual sparring was often intense, fueled by contrasting ideologies and research methodologies. However, such challenges only sharpened my arguments and honed my ability to defend my research with scientific rigor and unwavering conviction. I learned to anticipate their critiques, to preempt their objections, to present my findings with clarity and precision.

My research extended beyond the university walls. I spent summers assisting in expeditions to Loch Ness, working with sonar operators and underwater photographers. These expeditions weren't glamorous; they involved long days on the water, battling harsh weather conditions, and enduring the constant scrutiny of the media. But they provided invaluable firsthand experience, a deeper understanding of the loch's environment, and a chance to gather data directly from the source.

I collaborated with colleagues from other universities, experts in various fields ranging from geology and hydrology to image analysis and statistical modeling. Their expertise complemented my own, expanding the scope of my research and adding depth to my analyses. Working with these experts broadened my understanding of the intricacies of Loch Ness, revealing layers of complexity far beyond what I had initially anticipated.

The most challenging aspect of my research was balancing the scientific methodology with the intuitive understanding born from my childhood experience. The scientific method demands objectivity, a detachment from personal biases. Yet, the profound emotional connection to my initial sighting of Nessie remained a powerful force in my research, driving my passion and shaping my interpretations. I had to carefully navigate this delicate balance, ensuring that my personal experience did not compromise the rigor of my scientific work. This often meant engaging in rigorous self-critique, subjecting my own interpretations to intense scrutiny to ensure objectivity and eliminate bias.

My doctoral defense was an intense experience. The examining committee, a panel of seasoned professors, subjected my research to rigorous questioning, probing for weaknesses and inconsistencies. They challenged my methodology, scrutinized my data, and questioned my interpretations. The hours-long interrogation tested my knowledge, my resilience, and my ability to defend my work under pressure. But I had prepared thoroughly; I knew my research inside and out, and I was able to answer their questions with clarity and confidence.

The successful defense was more than an academic achievement; it was a vindication. It validated years of hard work, countless hours of research, and the unwavering pursuit of a truth that many had dismissed as fanciful. It proved that cryptozoology, despite the skepticism it faced, could be approached with rigorous scientific methodology, and that the pursuit of extraordinary phenomena was not necessarily a contradiction to scientific principles. The hard-earned doctorate was not just a symbol of academic achievement but a testament to the power of persistence, the importance of critical thinking, and the unwavering pursuit of truth, no matter how elusive or unconventional. It was the completion of the first phase of my journey, a stepping stone towards a more profound and perhaps even more extraordinary investigation. The path of uncovering Nessie's mysteries extended far beyond the halls of academia.

The phone call came on a blustery November evening, the wind howling a mournful tune outside my Inverness cottage. It was Hamish MacIntyre, a seasoned fisherman and a man whose word carried considerable weight in the close-knit community surrounding Loch Ness. His voice, usually booming with hearty laughter, was strained, almost hushed. "Skye," he said, his words clipped with urgency, "Ye need tae see this."

He'd found something – or rather, someone – during a late-night fishing trip. Not just an unusual ripple in the water, not just a fleeting shadow, but a substantial creature, unmistakable in its size and movement. He described it with the careful precision of a seasoned observer: a serpentine form, impossibly long, moving with a grace that defied its immense bulk. The water around it churned, creating a vortex that swallowed the smaller boats in its wake, and its dorsal fin, he claimed, resembled a massive, jagged obsidian blade piercing the surface. He'd only glimpsed it momentarily before a sudden, chilling fog enveloped the loch, swallowing the creature and obscuring his vision. It vanished as quickly as it had appeared, leaving behind an unsettling silence and a lingering unease in the pit of his stomach.

Hamish's account wasn't merely hearsay. He'd managed to capture a grainy video on his aging smartphone – a fleeting glimpse, mostly obscured by mist and the swirling water, but enough to ignite a spark of hope, a flicker of renewed conviction within me. The footage showed a dark, sinuous shape moving through the murky depths, a fleeting glimpse of a dorsal fin hinting at something enormous and powerful. The quality was poor, the lighting inadequate, but the sheer scale of the movement was undeniable. It was far too large to be any known species of aquatic life in Loch Ness.

This wasn't the blurry, ambiguous footage that often circulated online, dismissed as lens flares or playful otters. This felt different, more tangible, closer to the truth I'd spent years searching for. This was the missing link, the corroborating evidence that could finally push Nessie out of the realm of legend and into the realm of scientific possibility. The years spent in the university archives, poring over sonar data and eyewitness accounts, now felt like a purposeful preparation for this moment.

Within hours, I was on the road, my trusty Land Rover Defender bouncing along the uneven tracks leading to Hamish's home on the loch's northern shore. The anticipation was palpable, a mixture of excitement and nerves. This wasn't just another possible Nessie sighting; this felt like a turning point, a pivotal moment that could change everything. I'd spent years meticulously building my case, amassing evidence, presenting my findings to a skeptical scientific community. Now, the evidence had found me.

Hamish greeted me with a mug of steaming tea and a worried frown. The wind howled fiercely outside, mimicking the turmoil raging within him. He showed me the footage again, his eyes darting nervously to the window. He'd confided in no one else – the fear of ridicule, the fear of being labelled a fantasist, was etched on his weathered face.

We spent hours dissecting the video frame by frame, analyzing every pixel, every subtle shift in the water's surface. My years of image processing skills were put to the test. I used a variety of software to enhance the contrast, adjust the brightness, and filter out the noise. The results were tantalizing, though far from conclusive. The creature remained largely obscured, yet the scale of its movement, the disturbance in the water, and the shape of what appeared to be its fin were compelling.

Beyond the video, I interrogated Hamish about the details of his encounter. His recollections were vivid, his descriptions precise. He'd noticed a series of unusual disturbances in the water before the creature's appearance – strange, rhythmic pulses emanating from the depths. He'd dismissed it initially as some sort of geological phenomenon, but now, coupled with the sighting, it felt significant. He'd also reported a peculiar metallic scent in the air, a faint, almost electrical aroma that vanished as quickly as the creature itself.

The next morning, I contacted my team – a carefully selected group of experts I'd collaborated with during my doctoral studies. There was Dr. Eleanor Vance, a marine biologist specializing in sonar technology; Dr. Ben Carter, a geologist with a keen interest in underwater cave systems; and Liam O'Malley, a seasoned documentary filmmaker whose expertise was invaluable in documenting the expedition. I knew their skepticism would be formidable, but their skills were indispensable. I presented them with Hamish's testimony and the enhanced video footage.

Their initial reactions ranged from cautious interest to outright skepticism. Eleanor, ever the pragmatist, pointed out the limitations of the video evidence and suggested alternative explanations – large schools of fish, underwater currents, even a cleverly designed hoax. Ben, intrigued by Hamish's mention of unusual underwater sounds, highlighted the existence of a complex network of unexplored underwater caves beneath Loch Ness, suggesting that the creature might be utilizing these for shelter or navigation. Liam, however, was captivated by the potential story, his filmmaker's instinct already crafting narratives around the mysterious event.

Despite their varied responses, the undeniable fact remained: something significant had occurred. A creature of immense size and unusual mobility had been witnessed by a credible source. The evidence, though circumstantial, was compelling enough to warrant a thorough investigation. We decided to undertake a comprehensive sonar survey of the loch, focusing on the area where Hamish had made his sighting. We also planned to explore the network of underwater caves, a task that presented its own set of unique challenges.

The expedition was meticulously planned. We chartered a research vessel equipped with state-of-the-art sonar technology, and Eleanor meticulously calibrated the equipment, ensuring we obtained the highest quality data possible. Ben oversaw the selection of specialized diving equipment suitable for the exploration of the potentially hazardous underwater caves. Liam documented our every move, capturing the drama, the tension, and the sheer uncertainty of our mission. The weight of our purpose was palpable.

The initial sonar scans revealed little of interest. The loch's depths were a chaotic mix of geological formations, sediment plumes, and the ever-present presence of aquatic life. The vastness of the loch, the sheer volume of data we were processing, felt overwhelming. Days turned into nights as we scanned and rescanned, desperately searching for any sign, any anomaly that might suggest the presence of the elusive creature.

Just as despair began to creep in, a series of unusual sonar readings appeared on the screens. They were intermittent, sporadic, yet undeniably, there – deep, resonant pulses emanating from beneath the surface, resonating with the mysterious rhythm Hamish had described. The readings were concentrated within a specific area of the loch, near a submerged cliff face that marked the entrance to a previously unexplored cave system.

The discovery sent a wave of excitement through our team. This wasn't just random noise; this was evidence, a tangible indication that something extraordinary was lurking in the depths of Loch Ness. The mystery, rather than being solved, had deepened, becoming even more enthralling. The journey into the heart of the loch, and into the heart of Nessie's realm, had just begun. The next step was to explore the caves themselves. A risky and potentially hazardous step, but one we were now fully committed to taking. The renewed sighting had not simply reignited my obsession; it had transformed it into a burning determination, an all-consuming quest for the truth that lay hidden beneath the surface of Loch Ness.

The adrenaline from the sonar readings hadn't quite subsided when I began assembling my team. It wasn't just about finding Nessie; it was about proving her existence, understanding her connection to the strange phenomena Hamish had described, and exploring the implications of what that might mean for our understanding of the world. This wasn't a casual expedition; it was a carefully orchestrated scientific endeavor, albeit one shrouded in a veil of what many would consider fantastical elements. My team needed to be as diverse and capable as the challenges ahead.

First, there was Dr. Eleanor Vance, a marine biologist whose reputation preceded her. Her expertise lay in underwater acoustics and sonar technology, making her an invaluable asset in navigating the complexities of Loch Ness's depths. Eleanor, with her sharp intellect and unwavering pragmatism, was the anchor of our team. She possessed a dry wit that could cut through any tense situation, a vital counterpoint to my sometimes overzealous enthusiasm. Years spent analyzing sonar data in the icy waters of Antarctica had instilled in her a steely resolve and a meticulous attention to detail. Her skepticism, while initially frustrating, was essential – a crucial counterbalance to my own fervent belief in Nessie's existence. Her office, a meticulously organized sanctuary of scientific papers and advanced technological equipment, was a stark contrast to the chaotic energy that usually surrounded me. She approached every situation with a logical, methodical precision, a much-needed grounding force amongst the team.

Then came Dr. Ben Carter, a geologist whose specialty was the formation and exploration of underwater cave systems. He was a man of quiet intensity, his passion for his work radiating from him like a low hum. Ben's knowledge of subterranean formations was unparalleled. He'd spent years exploring the world's most challenging cave systems, developing a unique expertise in navigating treacherous underwater environments. He had a calm, almost meditative demeanor, a welcome contrast to the often frenetic energy of the rest of the team. His contributions to the team were invaluable, particularly in strategizing the exploration of the newly discovered underwater cave systems near the loch. His workspace was a fascinating blend of ancient geological maps and cutting-edge 3D modeling software; a representation of his ability to bridge the gap between historical knowledge and modern technology. He carried a quiet confidence, seemingly unfazed by the challenges ahead.

Liam O'Malley, our documentary filmmaker, brought a completely different dimension to the team. Liam wasn't just a technician; he was a storyteller, a master of visual narrative. His experience in capturing compelling footage in some of the world's most remote and dangerous locations was vital for documenting our expedition. He had a natural talent for capturing the raw emotions of any moment. He had an almost uncanny ability to weave a captivating narrative, even in the face of setbacks. He had the ability to translate complex scientific data into visually compelling stories. His office, more of a studio than a typical workspace, was a testament to his artistry. He was armed with several cameras and state-of-the-art editing equipment, capable of transforming even grainy footage into something mesmerizing.

The final member of our team was a somewhat unexpected addition: Dr. Anya Sharma, a physicist specializing in temporal anomalies. I had met Anya during a conference on unexplained phenomena a year earlier. Her work on the potential for localized temporal distortions, initially met with academic derision, had recently gained traction, particularly within the fringe community that studied cryptozoology. Her skepticism about Nessie initially mirrored Eleanor's, but her expertise added a crucial layer to our investigation. Anya's involvement was controversial, even within our team. Her theories, bordering on the edge of theoretical physics, were not easily accepted. Her introduction to the team was met with some unease; however, her calm demeanor, coupled with the unexpected clues she picked up while analyzing the video, soon swayed the others. Her office, if one could call it that, was a chaotic jumble of equations, diagrams, and complex mathematical models scribbled on whiteboards. She presented a unique perspective, pushing the boundaries of conventional scientific thought, a critical asset in exploring the potentially time-bending implications of Nessie's connection to the underground cave system.

The initial meetings took place in my Inverness cottage, a cozy, if somewhat cluttered, space filled with maps, research papers, and assorted Nessie memorabilia. The atmosphere was one of intense focus, a blend of scientific rigor and the palpable excitement of embarking on an extraordinary adventure. Each member, despite their diverse backgrounds, brought a unique skill set, and more importantly, an open mind to the possibilities. The initial skepticism didn't vanish completely, but it was tempered by a shared sense of wonder and a collective thirst for discovery.

Eleanor painstakingly analyzed the sonar data, creating detailed three-dimensional maps of the loch's floor, pinpointing potential areas of interest, and identifying previously unknown underwater structures. Ben, utilizing the latest geological survey techniques, created a comprehensive model of the cave system, highlighting potential access points and assessing the risks involved in exploration. Liam meticulously documented our progress, capturing not just the scientific details but also the human element, the camaraderie and the shared anxieties of the expedition. Anya, poring over the video footage, applied her expertise in temporal physics, searching for any evidence of anomalies that could explain the strange phenomena Hamish had described – the metallic scent, the rhythmic pulses, the sudden fog.

Days blurred into a flurry of activity. We spent hours poring over maps, analyzing data, and refining our strategies. We debated theories, challenged each other's assumptions, and collaboratively built a plan for a potentially dangerous, but ultimately rewarding, expedition. The discussions were lively, sometimes heated, but always respectful. There were disagreements, of course, clashes of personalities and differing approaches, but underlying it all was a shared commitment to uncovering the truth, whatever that might be. The combined expertise of the team was proving invaluable, building a synergy that surpassed individual brilliance. The possibility of rewriting history, of uncovering a hidden world beneath Loch Ness, galvanized us. We were no longer just a team of scientists; we were explorers, pioneers venturing into the unknown, guided by an ancient mystery and the flickering hope that our quest would reveal more than just a legend. The Nessie obsession, once solely mine, was now shared, a burning flame that united us. The expedition into the heart of the mystery was fast approaching; it was time to prepare for the unknown.

The final preparations felt less like a scientific expedition and more like a military operation. Each member had a specific role, a carefully defined task within the larger mission. Eleanor meticulously calibrated our underwater drones, ensuring their sonar systems were functioning at peak efficiency. She'd spent countless hours simulating the loch's conditions, testing the equipment's durability and range in a purpose-built tank in her lab, a miniature version of the vast, unpredictable underwater landscape awaiting us. Ben, meanwhile, meticulously mapped our planned route through the underwater cave system, utilizing the latest 3D modeling software to create a virtual replica. He identified potential hazards – unstable rock formations, submerged debris, unpredictable currents – and devised strategies to mitigate the risks. The detailed diagrams were spread across the table in my cottage, forming a complex, interwoven tapestry of potential routes and escape paths, a testament to his meticulous planning. Liam, ever the pragmatist, checked and rechecked his equipment, ensuring his cameras were waterproof, his lighting systems were robust, and his backup power sources were fully charged. He even went so far as to prepare a second set of equipment, hidden safely in a waterproof container, in case of any unforeseen technical difficulties. He treated each piece of equipment as a precious piece of his storytelling puzzle, realizing that every second of footage captured would be critical in unraveling the greater mystery. Anya, ever the enigma, worked in relative isolation, her concentration unbroken by the organized chaos around her. She'd begun refining her temporal distortion detection algorithms, focusing on the rhythmic pulse and electromagnetic anomalies we'd detected in the sonar readings. The rhythmic pulse, she theorized, could be the key, an intricate signature resonating through time, a subtle tremor in the fabric of space-time itself. She worked late into the night, her whiteboard covered with complex equations and diagrams, her focus intense and unwavering.

The journey to Loch Ness began on a crisp autumn morning, the Scottish Highlands shrouded in a mist that clung to the hillsides like a spectral shroud. The air was crisp and carried the scent of pine and damp earth. Our expedition vehicle, a rugged, modified Land Rover, lumbered along the winding roads, its cargo hold packed with equipment and supplies. The journey, despite the picturesque scenery, was fraught with tension. The anticipation was palpable, a mixture of excitement and apprehension. We'd spent months preparing, but there was no guarantee of success. The unpredictability of the Scottish weather, the treacherous terrain, and the sheer enigma of our quest hung heavy in the air.

Reaching the loch, the sheer scale of the water overwhelmed us, its surface a mirror reflecting the brooding sky. The air was heavy with a chill that seeped into our bones. The wind carried the cry of gulls, a discordant counterpoint to the stillness of the water. The initial attempt to launch the underwater drones proved more challenging than anticipated. The strong currents near the suspected portholes, the points of entry to the underground cave system, made deploying the drones a risky maneuver. Eleanor, with her years of experience, guided the process with steely precision, making minute adjustments to compensate for the unpredictable movement of the water. Several attempts were required; each deployment met with a struggle against the strong currents. Finally, after several tense moments, the drones were successfully launched, their sonar systems sending pulses into the murky depths, the underwater equivalents of our initial explorations of the cave system.

The sonar readings, initially fragmented and unreliable due to the turbulent water, slowly began to paint a more detailed picture of the loch's floor. The underwater cave system was even more extensive than our preliminary surveys had indicated. Ben, monitoring the data, excitedly pointed out a new, previously undetected passage, a narrow fissure hidden behind a massive rock formation. This discovery was significant; it suggested a deeper, more complex network of caves extending far beyond the loch itself. The possibility of uncovering an extensive network of hidden underground tunnels and chambers filled us with a renewed sense of excitement and urgency. This was more than just a mystery; it was a gateway to a hidden world beneath Loch Ness. The thrill of discovery was both exhilarating and nerve-wracking, a constant reminder of the scale and the risks associated with the expedition. The unpredictable nature of the terrain and the unknown depths of the loch had already presented its initial challenges, a clear indication that this journey would be fraught with unforeseen problems.

Our first attempt to enter the cave system resulted in a setback. One of the drones became entangled in submerged debris, its sonar signal abruptly ceasing. Eleanor and Ben quickly devised a recovery plan, meticulously plotting a course for a remotely operated submersible. The submersible, a small, highly maneuverable craft, was equipped with a robotic arm to disentangle the drone. The recovery operation was tense; the visibility was near zero, and the currents were strong and unpredictable. Liam, his cameras ready, captured the entire event, his footage a testament to the challenges we were facing, the unforeseen problems that added to the unpredictable nature of the exploration. The submersible mission, successful in recovering the drone, consumed most of the day; the recovery efforts significantly delayed our entry into the underground cave system, reminding us of the unforgiving reality of our journey.

As the day faded and the loch was overtaken by a growing darkness, the wind grew stronger, whipping across the surface of the water. The cold seeped deep into our bones. We retreated to our temporary base, a cluster of caravans situated on the edge of the loch. The atmosphere was subdued, laced with a growing sense of unease. The initial challenges were a sharp reminder of the scale of the task ahead and the unforgiving nature of the Scottish wilderness. The initial success in mapping the underground system was quickly overshadowed by the difficulties we'd encountered. Despite setbacks, the unwavering determination and excitement fueled by the discovery of the new passage propelled the team forward, determined to continue the exploration regardless of the obstacles ahead. The mystery of Loch Ness, far from being solved, had deepened, revealing itself to be a more complex and challenging enigma than any of us could have initially imagined. The next day, armed with a renewed sense of purpose and a revised plan, we would return to the loch, ready to face the unknown depths of Loch Ness, the mysterious underwater cave system, and whatever mysteries lay hidden within its depths. The initial challenges were simply the prelude to the far greater adventure.

Chapter 2

The Hidden Caves

The next morning dawned grey and windswept, mirroring the mood in our temporary camp. The recovered drone, thankfully undamaged beyond a few scrapes, hummed quietly, its sonar already recalibrated and ready for deployment. The revised plan, meticulously crafted by Ben, focused on a more cautious approach to the newly discovered passage. We'd learned a valuable lesson the previous day: the Loch Ness depths weren't simply an aquatic environment; they were a treacherous labyrinth, demanding respect and meticulous planning.

This time, instead of deploying the drones from the surface, we opted for a more direct approach. The submersible, christened 'Nessie's Eye' by Liam – a testament to his ever-present sense of dramatic flair – would carry Eleanor and me into the cave system. Ben and Anya would remain on the surface, monitoring the sonar data and providing support. Liam, ever the documentary filmmaker, would operate a remote camera system, relaying live footage of our underwater exploration.

The descent was slow and deliberate. The submersible's powerful lights cut through the inky blackness of the water, revealing a world of surprising beauty and unexpected danger. Schools of fish, startled by our intrusion, darted away, their silver bodies flashing momentarily in the beams. The water was frigid, and the pressure increased steadily as we descended, a constant reminder of the immense weight of the loch pressing down on us.

As we approached the entrance to the cave system, the underwater landscape transformed dramatically. The relatively open expanse of the loch gave way to a claustrophobic tunnel, its walls lined with smooth, dark rocks that seemed to absorb the light. The sense of confinement was immediate, a palpable weight pressing in on us, accentuating the sense of isolation and the profound mystery that surrounded us.

Navigating the narrow passage was challenging, the submersible, despite its maneuverability, struggled to move freely through the tight spaces, its metal hull occasionally scraping against the cave walls, sending shivers down my spine. The silence, punctuated only by the hum of the submersible's engines and the occasional drip of water from the ceiling, was oppressive, a constant reminder of our isolation and the vast unknown surrounding us. The darkness felt ancient and impenetrable, a stark contrast to the more open waters we'd experienced initially.

The cave system extended far deeper than we had initially anticipated. The tunnels twisted and turned, leading us into chambers of varying sizes, some vast and echoing, others narrow and constricted. Stalactites, formed over millennia by dripping water, hung like eerie decorations from the ceilings, their sharp tips seemingly poised to impale us. The floor was uneven, covered in layers of silt and debris, a testament to the age and geological complexity of this hidden world. Each turn revealed a new challenge, a new obstacle to overcome, a new mystery to unravel. The thrill of discovery, once exhilarating, now felt tinged with a growing sense of unease.

The longer we explored, the more ominous the atmosphere became. The air, or rather the water, seemed to grow colder, a tangible chill that permeated the submersible's hull. The darkness intensified, obscuring even the strongest light, reducing our visibility to a mere few meters. Strange sounds echoed through the tunnels – low groans and rumbles that seemed to emanate from the very rocks themselves. These unsettling noises were neither the natural sounds of the water nor the usual sounds of a cave system; they were mysterious, deeply unsettling and had an almost supernatural quality.

In one particularly large cavern, we encountered an unexpected sight: a colossal fissure, splitting the cavern floor in two. The fissure extended deep into the earth, its darkness absolute and impenetrable. The sheer scale of it was awe-inspiring, but also terrifying. It felt like a gaping maw in the earth, a gateway to something profoundly ancient and unknown. The walls of the fissure seemed to shimmer slightly in the submersible's beam, their surfaces covered with strange, bioluminescent organisms that pulsed with an ethereal, otherworldly glow.

As we proceeded further into the cavern system, the sonar readings became increasingly erratic. Anya, monitoring the data on the surface, reported anomalies in the temporal distortion readings. The rhythmic pulse, the signature she'd been tracking, was growing stronger, more insistent. It was as though the very fabric of time itself was resonating within this hidden subterranean world. Her voice, relayed through the submersible's comms system, was laced with a mixture of excitement and apprehension. This was more than just a geological exploration; it was a journey into the heart of something that challenged our understanding of space and time.

The claustrophobia intensified, pushing against our mental endurance. The narrow passageways and the oppressive darkness were beginning to take their toll, increasing the growing sense of uneasiness and tension. The unexpected sounds echoing through the tunnels, along with the increasingly erratic sonar readings and the unusual temporal distortions, created a nightmarish atmosphere, as if we were intruding into a forbidden world. The discovery of the fissure had heightened the sense of foreboding, increasing our awareness of the unknown potential dangers lurking deeper inside this complex cave system.

We encountered several smaller chambers, some containing strange mineral formations, others filled with unusual aquatic life forms that seemed adapted to the extreme conditions of the deep, dark cave system. These creatures, unlike anything we'd seen before, seemed almost alien in their appearance, their bioluminescent bodies casting an eerie glow in the darkness. They moved with a strange grace, their movements seemingly governed by an intelligence that defied our understanding of aquatic life. These lifeforms, living in the extreme environment of the cave system, presented a clear indication of a previously unknown ecosystem. This further fueled our belief that there were still many unanswered questions and mysteries waiting to be discovered in the hidden depths of Loch Ness.

Our exploration was far from over. The cave system seemed endless, a labyrinthine network extending far beyond our initial estimations. The air (water) grew colder, the darkness deeper, the feeling of unease more pronounced. We were in the very heart of a hidden world, a world that seemed to defy explanation. The rhythmic pulse from Anya's readings was now almost deafening, a constant reminder of the temporal distortions warping the very fabric of reality within the cave system. It was clear we had only scratched the surface of a profound mystery. A mystery that threatened to change our understanding of the world, and perhaps even of time itself. As we continued deeper into the dark, damp interior of this hidden network of caves, the thrill of discovery was constantly overshadowed by a deep-seated sense of unease, a tangible feeling that we had stumbled upon something far more significant, and far more dangerous, than we could ever have imagined. The journey had only just begun, and the unknown depths of Loch Ness held secrets waiting to be revealed. The potential consequences of this expedition were far-reaching and still unknown.

Further, into the labyrinthine network, the submersible's lights illuminated a chamber unlike any we had encountered before. This wasn't a simple cavern; it was a vast, echoing space, its dimensions seemingly defying the confines of the surrounding rock. The walls, instead of the smooth, dark rock we'd become accustomed to, were intricately carved, adorned with bas-reliefs depicting strange, almost otherworldly creatures and symbols that defied any known language or culture. The carvings were weathered, worn smooth by the relentless passage of time and the ceaseless flow of water, yet they still held a certain majesty, an undeniable power that resonated even through the submersible's thick hull.

Eleanor gasped, her voice barely audible over the comms system. "Ben, Anya, you have to see this. It's... it's incredible."

The images relayed by Liam's remote camera system confirmed the breathtaking sight. The carvings extended across vast swathes of the cavern wall, telling a silent, intricate story stretching back millennia. The figures depicted were humanoid, yet possessed features that hinted at something beyond human: elongated limbs, oversized heads, and eyes that seemed to glow faintly even in the submersible's harsh light. They were engaged in activities that appeared both ritualistic and technological, manipulating devices that looked oddly familiar yet utterly alien.

Among the carvings were symbols – glyphs, perhaps – that repeated themselves in seemingly random patterns. They weren't simply decorative; they possessed a strange, almost hypnotic quality, as if they were vibrating with a hidden energy. Eleanor, with her background in ancient languages, attempted to decipher them, but found herself utterly baffled. They bore no resemblance to any known language or script, ancient or modern. They were unique, enigmatic, hinting at a civilization lost to time, a history buried deep beneath the waters of Loch Ness.

Scattered across the cavern floor, amid the silt and debris, were artifacts – remnants of this lost civilization. These weren't mere fragments; they were remarkably well-preserved objects, their material composition defying the harsh conditions of the underwater cave. We carefully maneuvered the submersible, using the manipulator arms to gently collect samples.

The first object we recovered was a small, metallic sphere, perfectly smooth and polished, etched with the same enigmatic glyphs we'd seen on the cave walls. It felt strangely warm to the touch, radiating a subtle hum that could be felt through the submersible's glove. Ben, ever the scientist, immediately initiated a series of tests, but the sphere's composition defied his analysis. It wasn't any known metal or alloy, exhibiting properties that suggested it was far beyond our current technological capabilities.

Next, we discovered a series of intricately carved stone tablets, covered in the same alien glyphs. These tablets seemed to depict a complex astronomical chart, detailing constellations unknown to modern science, suggesting a level of astronomical understanding that far surpassed anything we possessed. Their preservation was astounding; the carvings were sharp and precise, as if they'd been created only recently.

The most striking artifact, however, was a large, crystalline structure that rested in the center of the cavern. It resembled a gigantic prism, its facets shimmering with an internal light that pulsed with a faint rhythm, echoing the temporal distortions Anya had detected. The crystal emanated a palpable energy, a hum that resonated not only through the water but also seemed to resonate within our very being. It was breathtakingly beautiful, yet unnervingly powerful. Its presence alone suggested a potent source of energy or information, hidden within its enigmatic crystalline structure.

Approaching the crystalline structure, the submersible's sonar began to produce erratic readings, the temporal distortions intensifying. Anya's voice crackled through the comms system, her tone filled with a mixture of awe and fear. "The temporal anomalies are peaking. I've never seen anything like this before! It's like the structure is... warping time itself."

Liam, ever the filmmaker, captured stunning close-up footage of the crystal. The light emanating from within the structure shifted and changed, revealing complex patterns and symbols that mirrored those found on the sphere and the tablets. It was as if the crystal itself was communicating, transmitting information beyond our comprehension.

As we attempted to collect a sample from the crystal, a strange, pulsating energy field enveloped the submersible. The lights flickered, and the comms system sputtered, losing contact with the surface team. For a brief moment, the world around us seemed to distort, the images blurring, the sounds warping into an unsettling cacophony. Then, as suddenly as it had begun, the anomaly ceased, and communication was restored.

Ben's voice, filled with apprehension, crackled through the comms system. "What happened down there? Your readings are off the charts! And the temporal distortion... it's unprecedented."

We cautiously retreated from the crystal, a newfound respect for its power and its potential dangers. The artifacts we had collected were enough for now, more than enough to confirm that we had stumbled upon something truly extraordinary, a hidden chapter in the history of our planet, a lost civilization that possessed a technology and understanding far beyond our own. The implications were staggering.

Leaving the cavern, the journey back to the surface felt surreal. The eerie silence of the cave system had been replaced by a newfound appreciation of the world we had left behind. The weight of our discovery pressed down upon us, a sense of responsibility mixing with the profound mystery we had uncovered.

As we emerged from the depths of Loch Ness, into the grey light of the Scottish dawn, it became clear that our adventure had only just begun. The ancient artifacts, the cryptic symbols, the enigmatic crystal – these were merely clues, breadcrumbs leading us further into a mystery that was far grander, far more profound, and potentially far more dangerous, than we could have possibly imagined. We still had much to learn, much to uncover, as the full implications of our findings continued to sink in. The journey into this hidden world had revealed a glimpse of a forgotten history, a history shrouded in mystery and bound with the potential for significant revelations. Our investigation had just scratched the surface, leaving a trail of unanswered questions and the tantalizing promise of more discoveries to come. The fate of the unknown remained unknown, but the clues we possessed hinted at the potential for significant paradigm shifts in our understanding of the past and the present.

The recovered artifacts were carefully documented and cataloged, awaiting further analysis. Their implications were vast, suggesting a civilization far more advanced than any we knew, one capable of manipulating time and harnessing energies that lay beyond our current comprehension. The mystery of the Loch Ness Monster, once our singular focus, now paled in comparison to the far greater enigma we had uncovered, the connection between the creature, the ancient artifacts, and the temporal anomalies remained a central mystery, driving our team to uncover its secrets. It became clear that the story of Loch Ness was far more expansive and far more significant than we had initially conceived. We were standing on the precipice of a profound discovery, a discovery that had the potential to reshape our understanding of history and the very fabric of reality itself. The questions that now demanded answers were exponentially greater than our initial exploration, and the path forward was unclear. Yet, we were propelled by a newfound drive, driven to explore the potential impact of this forgotten civilization and its mysteries. The future held the potential for extraordinary revelations, but also unforeseen challenges and perils. We knew our adventure was far from over. The thrill of exploration and the fear of the unknown were intertwined, driving us forward into the depths of a still-unraveling mystery.

The next day, we all were excited to actually go back no matter what the consequences would be.

The submersible's powerful lights cut through the inky blackness, revealing a narrow passage barely wide enough for our vessel. The walls pressed in, slick with moisture and chillingly cold against the submersible's hull. Anya, monitoring the temporal anomalies, reported a slight increase in the distortions, a subtle warping of time around us, almost imperceptible yet undeniably present. The air, or rather, the water, crackled with an unseen energy, a palpable sense of unease settling over the team.

This wasn't the vast, echoing chamber we'd left behind; this was a claustrophobic, serpentine tunnel, twisting and turning in ways that seemed to defy logic. Liam, ever vigilant with his cameras, recorded the journey, the footage showing the cramped confines of our passage, the walls closing in around us. The silence was broken only by the hum of the submersible's engines and the occasional creak of the hull as it navigated the uneven terrain.

Suddenly, the submersible shuddered violently, throwing us against our restraints. A low groan echoed through the hull, a sound that spoke of immense pressure and shifting rock. Ben, his eyes glued to the sonar readings, swore under his breath. "We've hit something," he announced, his voice strained. "And it's big."

The sonar displayed a massive obstruction ahead, a wall of rock that appeared to have shifted, blocking our path. We tried maneuvering, attempting to find an alternative route, but the tunnel was impassable. We were trapped.

The air – the water – grew colder, and a strange, viscous substance began to coat the submersible's viewing dome. It was dark, almost black, and it seemed to pulse with a faint, internal light. Anya's readings spiked, the temporal distortions intensifying dramatically. "This is... this is unlike anything I've ever encountered," she gasped, her voice trembling slightly. "The temporal field is fluctuating wildly. I'm getting readings that suggest... localized time shifts, mini rips in the fabric of space-time."

Just then, a low growl reverberated through the water, a sound so deep and resonant that it seemed to vibrate in our very bones. The lights flickered, and the submersible shook again, more violently this time. Through the murky, viscous substance coating the dome, we saw it: a pair of enormous, glowing eyes, peering into the submersible, their gaze intense, intelligent, and utterly terrifying.

It was immense, a creature of nightmare, its form obscured by the darkness and the viscous substance, but its size and power were undeniable. It filled the tunnel, its presence a suffocating weight, a palpable sense of ancient, primal power. The creature let out another growl, a sound that was both a threat and a warning.

Ben frantically tried to reverse the submersible, but the creature seemed to be blocking our escape. It pressed against the submersible, its weight immense, the hull groaning under the strain. We were trapped, cornered, at the mercy of this behemoth that seemed to emanate from the very fabric of the earth, from the deepest recesses of this hidden world.

Eleanor, ever resourceful, suggested we try using the submersible's sonic emitter. Perhaps a high-frequency sound could disorient the creature long enough for us to escape. Ben cautiously activated the emitter, sending a pulse of high-frequency sound through the water. The creature recoiled, its glowing eyes flaring with anger, but it didn't retreat. It merely shifted its position, its immense form still pressing against the hull.

The temporal distortions intensified, reaching levels that were alarming even for Anya. The submersible's instruments went haywire, the lights flashing erratically, the comms system sputtering. The walls of the tunnel seemed to ripple and shift, as if they were being pulled and stretched by some unseen force.

Suddenly, the creature lunged, its enormous form striking the submersible with terrifying force. The hull creaked and groaned under the assault, its structure threatening to collapse. We were tossed around violently, the lights plunging into darkness before flickering back to life. The submersible's emergency lights illuminated a gaping crack in the hull, water pouring in.

We were sinking.

Against all odds, Ben managed to regain control of the submersible, firing the thrusters with everything he had. The submersible lurched forward, just narrowly avoiding complete destruction. But the creature was still close, its presence a chilling reminder of its power, its terrifying might.

As we escaped the immediate danger, the temporal distortions subsided, but not entirely. We pushed onward, the damaged hull leaking, our escape a desperate, perilous race against the mounting pressure and the unknown dangers that still lurked within this submerged labyrinth. The creature, the ancient artifacts, the temporal anomalies – it all came together, a confluence of mysteries that challenged our understanding of the world, of reality itself. We were trapped in a nightmarish scenario where the very fabric of time itself seemed to be against us.

The journey continued, each meter we covered fraught with peril. The tunnel was unstable, its walls crumbling and collapsing. The submersible lurched and swayed, water seeping in through the damaged hull. Our escape was no longer a simple mission; it became a desperate fight for survival against the elements, against the confines of this hidden world, and against the powerful, enigmatic creatures that inhabited it. The fear of being trapped forever in this claustrophobic, treacherous environment was palpable. Each creak of the hull, each tremor of the ground, sent shivers down our spines. We were playing against time, each second critical as the water relentlessly poured in.

The experience in the claustrophobic confines of the tunnels changed us, leaving each of us marked by the near-death experience. We were shaken, traumatized by the sheer power of the creature and the terrifying nature of the environment. The journey was a test of our courage, our resilience, and our determination. This close encounter reinforced the daunting reality of our mission, highlighting the risks involved in our exploration.

As we finally emerged into a larger cavern, the massive scale of the cave system and the many tunnels branching off in every direction took our breath away. We all got out of the submersible, which revealed a larger cavern. This larger cavern was remarkably less threatening than the tunnels we had just passed. The lingering effects of our terrifying encounter spurred us on to reach the surface. Even though the path ahead remained unclear and fraught with danger, the hope of escaping, of revealing our findings to the world, fueled our resolve. We were bruised, but not broken. Our mission had just become infinitely more dangerous, yet the stakes were now higher than ever. The allure of uncovering the secrets of this hidden world was now intertwined with a profound desire for survival.

The path ahead was unclear, the future uncertain, but one thing was sure: our adventure was far from over. We had survived, but we were changed. And the secrets hidden within the depths of Loch Ness remained tantalizingly out of reach, beckoning us to continue our exploration, even knowing the immeasurable risks involved. The mystery deepened, driving us toward a culmination that could change our world and our very understanding of existence. The weight of our discovery and the weight of our survival were now our two guiding stars as we continued onward.

The cavern echoed with the drip, drip, drip of water, a counterpoint to the frantic thump-thump-thump of my own heart. The air hung heavy with the scent of damp earth and something else... something ancient, something indefinably other. Behind me, the figures on the wall, huddled, their faces illuminated by the beams of our headlamps, a mixture of apprehension and fascination etched onto their features. We were surrounded by symbols, carved into the rock face, a language older than history itself.

This wasn't just geological formation; this was deliberate, meticulous craftsmanship. The glyphs were intricate, interwoven with a precision that suggested immense knowledge and skill. They weren't haphazard scratches; they were carefully planned, their placement suggesting a deliberate arrangement, a hidden code waiting to be unlocked.

My heart pounded with a mixture of excitement and trepidation. This was it. This was the moment I'd been working towards, the culmination of years of research, years of painstaking study of ancient languages, forgotten dialects, and esoteric symbology. This was the key to understanding the enigma of Loch Ness, the key to deciphering the mysteries of this hidden world.

I knelt before the wall, my fingers tracing the cool, smooth surface of the rock. The symbols were predominantly circular and linear, a combination of spirals, interconnected loops, and straight lines etched with astonishing precision. Some resembled constellations, others evoked images of aquatic creatures, and still others defied easy interpretation. They seemed to shimmer with an inner light, as if infused with an ancient energy.

Liam, ever the pragmatist, cautiously approached, his camera whirring softly. "What do you think they are, Skye?" he asked, his voice a hushed whisper in the echoing cavern.

"I believe they're a form of proto-writing," I replied, my voice barely above a breath. "A system of symbols predating any known written language. Their complexity suggests a highly developed civilization, one capable of advanced mathematics and astronomy."

Anya, our temporal physicist, stepped closer, her eyes wide with wonder. "The energy readings here are off the charts," she murmured. "It's like... the rock itself is resonating with something. There's a subtle temporal distortion emanating from the symbols themselves."

Ben, our seasoned geologist, examined the rock face with his expert eye. "The age of this is astonishing," he said, his voice filled with awe. "It's far older than anything we've previously encountered. This isn't just some cave system; this is a monument, a record of something incredible."

Eleanor, our tech expert, began to meticulously photograph the symbols, capturing every detail with her high-resolution camera. Her quiet efficiency provided a stark contrast to the thrill and trepidation pulsing through the rest of us. We were standing at the brink of a profound discovery, a moment that could rewrite history as we know it.

I began to work, my mind racing as I tried to decipher the cryptic messages. The glyphs themselves seemed to shift and rearrange before my eyes, as if they were alive, responding to my concentration. I recognized elements of various ancient languages: Proto-Indo-European, Sumerian cuneiform, Egyptian hieroglyphs, even hints of something that seemed to predate even them. It was a mind-bending combination, a complex cipher that required not only linguistic skill but also a deep understanding of the underlying cosmology implied within the symbols.

Hours bled into each other as we worked. The flickering beams of our lamps cast long, dancing shadows across the cavern walls, enhancing the mystical feel of the place. We were surrounded by the whispers of ages past, the echoes of a forgotten civilization. The silence was broken only by the scratching of my pen on my notepad, the soft clicks of Eleanor's camera, and the occasional murmured comment from one of the team.

I focused on a particular cluster of symbols, a recurring motif that seemed to be central to the entire system. It was a spiral, intertwined with a series of lines that resembled constellations. My mind raced, my intuition leading me down a path that felt both familiar and alien. I recalled a forgotten passage from a Sumerian tablet, a description of a celestial event, a conjunction of planets that only occurred once every several millennia.

Could this be a star chart, a celestial map? A guide to something... somewhere? The thought sent a shiver down my spine. The possibility of time travel, once a wild theory, now felt chillingly plausible. These weren't just symbols; they were keys to a vast, unknown universe, hinting at dimensions beyond human comprehension. The more I looked, the more convinced I became. The symbols weren't merely a language; they were a blueprint, a guide to a specific point in time and space.

The spiral seemed to represent a cyclical process, a return to a specific point. The intersecting lines represented the celestial bodies, their positions marking a unique astronomical event. The interconnectedness suggested a convergence, a point of intersection in space-time. The symbols were more than just a map; they were a navigation system, a pathway to a different era.

As I worked, the temporal distortions intensified. Anya's instruments registered unusual fluctuations, the air around us shimmering faintly. The feeling of unease, already present, intensified. It felt as if we weren't just deciphering symbols; we were opening a door to another world hidden beneath the waters of Loch Ness, a world that was both incredibly ancient and possibly incredibly close. The temporal shifts were becoming more pronounced, a tangible reminder of the power we were wielding, the dangerous knowledge we were uncovering.

I traced the lines again, my fingers lightly caressing the cold stone. I felt a strange pull, a resonance, as if the symbols themselves were speaking to me, sharing their secrets in a language older than words. The air vibrated with energy, a tangible hum that seemed to resonate with the deepest parts of my being. This wasn't just an intellectual exercise; it was a communion, a connection to a forgotten past that held the key to our future.

The intensity of my concentration intensified the temporal distortions. A faint hum filled the air, a vibration that resonated within my bones. I could almost feel the pull, the shifting of the fabric of space-time, the very ground seeming to tremble beneath our feet. The glyphs seemed to pulse with an inner light, their patterns shifting and swirling, their message unfolding before my very eyes.

Slowly, painstakingly, I deciphered the final element, a single, solitary symbol positioned at the heart of the spiral. It represented a date, a specific point in time, an intersection of celestial bodies that corresponded to a point far beyond the present, a point in the distant past, a window opening into another age. My breath caught in my throat. We had found it. We had found the gateway. The weight of the discovery pressed down on me, the immensity of the implications staggering. This was the culmination of years of research, the final piece of the puzzle. Our journey had just become exponentially more dangerous, and exponentially more thrilling. The hidden caves had revealed their secrets, but those secrets held the key to mysteries far greater than we could have ever imagined.

The air crackled with an unseen energy, a tangible hum that resonated deep within my chest. The symbols, once static carvings in the rock, now pulsed with an inner light, their patterns shifting and swirling as if alive. The faint scent of ozone filled the air, a sharp contrast to the damp earth smell that had previously dominated the cavern. Anya's temporal distortion meter screamed, its needle spinning wildly beyond its maximum reading. The ground beneath our feet trembled, a low, guttural rumble that seemed to emanate from deep within the earth itself.

Liam, ever the pragmatist, swallowed hard, his usually confident demeanor replaced by a look of stark apprehension. "This... this is more than just ancient writing," he stammered, his voice barely audible above the growing hum. "This is... something else entirely."

Ben, his geologist's intuition honed over decades of fieldwork, ran a hand over the pulsating rock face. "The geological activity... it's unprecedented," he breathed, his eyes wide with a mixture of awe and terror. "The rock itself is... vibrating. It's like the entire cavern is about to... shift."

Eleanor, usually unflappable, frantically checked her equipment, her fingers flying across her keyboard. "The energy readings are off the charts," she reported, her voice tight with anxiety. "It's not just temporal distortion; there's... something else. Something... extraterrestrial."

The revelation hung in the air, heavy and suffocating. Extraterrestrial. The word, once confined to the realms of science fiction, now held a chillingly real weight in this ancient, echoing cavern. My own heart pounded in my chest, a frantic drumbeat against the background hum. The symbols, their meaning now fully understood, felt less like a historical artifact and more like a key, a gateway to something... other.

The final symbol, the one at the heart of the spiral, pulsed with an intensified light, its brilliance piercing the gloom of the cavern. It wasn't just a date; it was a coordinate, a precise location in space-time. A precise location that was not just somewhere in the past, but potentially... somewhere else entirely. The implications were staggering. We weren't just looking at a historical artifact; we were gazing into a cosmic portal, a window into a reality beyond our comprehension.

The tremor intensified, the ground shaking violently. Dust rained down from the cavern ceiling, coating us in a fine layer of ancient earth. The air crackled with energy, the hum growing louder, more intense, until it felt as if our eardrums were about to burst. A low, guttural growl echoed through the cavern, a sound that sent shivers down my spine. It wasn't a geological sound; it was something... organic. Something... immense.

Fear, raw and visceral, snaked through me, but it was quickly replaced by a surge of adrenaline-fueled excitement. This was it. This was the moment we'd been working towards, the culmination of years of research, years of chasing shadows and whispers. We were on the verge of a discovery that could rewrite history, a discovery that could change the world as we knew it.

Suddenly, the light from the central symbol intensified, casting a brilliant, ethereal glow across the cavern walls. The symbols themselves shimmered, their patterns shifting and rearranging themselves before our eyes, the glyphs seeming to writhe and twist like living things. A vortex of shimmering energy began to form at the heart of the spiral, a swirling maelstrom of light and color, its edges shimmering with an otherworldly luminescence.

Anya gasped, her eyes wide with a mixture of fear and fascination. "The gateway... it's opening," she whispered, her voice barely audible above the growing hum. "It's... it's a tear in the fabric of space-time."

The air around the vortex crackled with energy, the temperature rising sharply. A strange, almost musical hum filled the air, a sound that vibrated deep within our very bones. The cavern itself seemed to breathe, the rock walls pulsating with a life of their own. The air shimmered and distorted, creating strange, surreal images that danced before our eyes.

Liam, despite his fear, reached for his camera, capturing images of the opening gateway. The photos showed a swirling vortex of light, a chaotic maelstrom of colors and patterns that defied easy description. It was beautiful, terrifying, and utterly mesmerizing.

Ben, his geologist's mind struggling to comprehend the impossibility of it all, muttered, "It's... warping the space around it. It's defying the laws of physics as we understand them."

Eleanor, ever the pragmatist, checked her instruments, but they were rendered useless, overwhelmed by the sheer power of the energy radiating from the vortex. The readings were off the scale, far beyond anything she had ever witnessed. This was far beyond just a temporal distortion; it was a dimensional shift, a tearing of the fabric of reality itself.

As the vortex continued to grow, a sense of anticipation and dread filled the air. We stood on the precipice of the unknown, ready to step through a doorway that led to a time and place beyond our wildest imaginings. The whispers of the past, the echoes of a forgotten civilization, were now becoming a tangible reality. The journey that had begun with a childhood fascination with the Loch Ness Monster, with the study of ancient languages and forgotten symbology, had finally led us here, to the gateway.

The hum intensified, reaching a crescendo that seemed to shake the very foundations of the earth. The air shimmered, the light intensified, and then, with a sudden rush of wind and a blinding flash of light, the vortex expanded, pulling us towards its center. We were no longer just observers; we were participants. We were being drawn into the heart of the mystery, into the very fabric of the unknown.

The last thing I saw before we plunged into the swirling vortex of light was the immense, serpentine form of a creature emerging from the depths of the opening, its eyes glowing with an ancient, otherworldly intelligence. Nessie. The legendary monster of Loch Ness. But this was no mere myth; this was something far greater, something far more ancient, something that held the key to unlocking the mysteries of time, space, and the universe itself. Our adventure had truly begun. The gateway had opened, and we were about to step through. The question wasn't if we were ready, but if we would ever be the same again.

Chapter 3

UFO Encounters

The vortex spat us out, not into a different time, but into a different... dimension? The swirling chaos subsided, replaced by the chilling stillness of a star-strewn Highland night. But this wasn't the night sky I knew. The stars were different, brighter, closer, arranged in constellations utterly alien to anything charted in human astronomy. The air hummed with an unfamiliar energy, a low thrumming that vibrated in my bones. Gone was the earthy scent of the cave, replaced by a sharp, metallic tang that prickled my nostrils.

Liam, ever the documentarian, frantically clicked his camera, capturing the impossibly bright, almost hallucinatory expanse above us. Ben, despite his initial shock, was already reaching for his geological hammer, tapping a nearby rock formation. It responded with a hollow, metallic clang, unlike any natural stone I had ever encountered. Anya, her face pale but her eyes shining with intense fascination, adjusted her temporal distortion meter. It remained stubbornly unresponsive, registering only a flatline—as if time itself had ceased to exist in this place.

Eleanor, however, let out a gasp, her eyes fixed on a point in the sky. "Look!" she whispered, her voice barely audible above the humming air.

Above us, a series of lights danced across the inky blackness. They weren't the steady twinkle of distant stars, but pulsating orbs of light, shifting in color and intensity with an eerie synchronicity. Some were a deep, throbbing red, others a brilliant, almost painful blue. A few pulsed with a sickly green light that seemed to drain the color from everything around it. They moved with impossible grace, defying the laws of physics as we understood them – accelerating, decelerating, changing direction instantaneously. They were not birds, not weather phenomena. These were... something else. Something alien.

The lights began to coalesce, forming intricate patterns across the sky, creating geometric shapes that shifted and rearranged themselves before our very eyes. One moment, it was a perfect cube; the next, a twisting spiral; then a multifaceted starburst. They were beautiful, mesmerizing, and deeply unnerving. The air crackled with energy, the humming intensifying, becoming a constant, throbbing pulse that threatened to overwhelm our senses.

Liam, despite his fear, continued to film, his camera struggling to capture the sheer brilliance and strangeness of the spectacle. He muttered something about lens flares and atmospheric disturbances, but I could see in his eyes the same awe and apprehension that consumed the rest of us.

"It's... it's like they're communicating," Ben whispered, his gaze fixed on the lights, his voice almost reverent. "The patterns... they're too complex, too precise to be random. It's like a language."

Eleanor, ever the scientist, was already attempting to analyze the light patterns with her spectrometer, but the readings were chaotic, nonsensical. The light itself seemed to be defying conventional scientific analysis. "The spectral signature... it's unlike anything I've ever encountered," she murmured, her brow furrowed in concentration. "There's... there's energy signatures intertwined with the light, like... coded messages."

The display intensified, the lights growing brighter, the patterns more intricate. A low, humming sound emanated from the lights themselves, a complex melody that resonated deep within our very beings. It was a sound that seemed to penetrate our very souls, evoking a strange sense of both fear and profound understanding, feeling of recognition and of ancient memories stirring within us.

Then, just as suddenly as it had begun, the display ceased. The lights blinked out, leaving us in the inky blackness of the alien night, the silence punctuated only by the faint, persistent hum that seemed to permeate the very fabric of reality itself. The metallic tang in the air remained, and the strange rock beneath our feet still resonated with a subtle, alien energy.

The abrupt silence was almost more terrifying than the spectacle itself. The absence of the lights left a void in the cosmos, a blank canvas that somehow felt more threatening than the swirling patterns and pulsating orbs that had just danced before our eyes.

Anya broke the silence, her voice trembling slightly. "What... what was that?"

Liam, still clutching his camera, shook his head slowly. "I... I don't know. I've never seen anything like it."

Ben, his gaze still fixed on the now empty sky, murmured, "They... they observed us. And then they left."

Eleanor, her expression thoughtful, added, "The energy signatures... they were definitely attempting to communicate. But the message... it was beyond our current ability to decipher."

A chilling realization washed over me. We weren't just searching for Nessie; we were stumbling upon something far greater, something that defied our understanding of the universe. The Loch Ness Monster, the ancient cave, the temporal anomalies... they were all connected, all part of a larger, more complex puzzle. A puzzle that might lead to the rewriting of history itself. The encounter with the strange lights had only deepened the mystery. What had we seen? Who – or

***what* – had been observing us?**

The implications were staggering. If this was a form of extraterrestrial communication, what were their intentions? Were they benevolent or malevolent? What other secrets lay hidden in this strange, alien landscape?

The questions haunted us as we trekked back to the cave, the image of the pulsating lights still seared into our minds. The hum, the metallic scent, the strange rock formations – all served as constant reminders of our incredible encounter. Our adventure had taken an unexpected turn, veering from the realm of cryptozoology into the far more enigmatic territory of extraterrestrial contact. The path ahead was shrouded in uncertainty, but one thing was certain: our search for Nessie had become something far greater, far more profound. We were no longer just searching for a monster; we were on the verge of uncovering secrets that could change humanity's understanding of its place in the universe. And with every step we took towards unraveling the mystery of the Loch Ness Monster, we were drawing closer to an even greater enigma: the mystery of the universe itself.

The silence of our return journey was broken only by the occasional rustle of leaves and the crunch of gravel under our boots. Each of us was lost in our own thoughts, processing the impossible events of the past few hours. The images of the pulsating lights, the complex patterns, the eerie silence that followed, all swirled in our minds, creating a maelstrom of confusion, wonder, and apprehension.

Liam, ever the pragmatist, tried to rationalize the experience, mumbling about unusual atmospheric conditions and potential optical illusions, but even he couldn't fully dismiss the evidence before his eyes. The videos he had captured were irrefutable proof of something extraordinary, something that defied explanation.

Ben, the geologist, found solace in the familiarity of the rock formations, his hands tracing the contours of the ancient stones. But even the solidity of the earth beneath his feet couldn't entirely quell the sense of unease that lingered in the air. The strange metallic clang of the rocks, the lingering hum in the air, these were tangible reminders of the alien landscape we had just experienced.

Anya, despite her initial fear, was fueled by a sense of profound curiosity. Her temporal distortion meter had remained stubbornly silent during the spectacle, suggesting that the lights operated outside the constraints of conventional space and time. This only strengthened her belief that we were on the verge of a truly revolutionary discovery.

Eleanor, ever analytical, continued to pore over the data she had collected, her fingers flying across her keyboard. She believed that the energy signatures intertwined with the light contained a hidden message, a code that could unlock the secrets of the extraterrestrial intelligence that had observed us.

My own mind raced, attempting to connect the disparate pieces of the puzzle: the ancient cave, the symbols, Nessie, the temporal anomalies, and now, the extraterrestrial lights. The connections were not immediately obvious, yet I felt intuitively that they were all inextricably linked.

As we reached the entrance to the cave system, the faint light of dawn began to break over the Scottish Highlands. The sky was a pale, ethereal blue, a stark contrast to the otherworldly spectacle we had witnessed just hours before. The normalcy of the landscape was a jarring contrast to the extraordinary events we had experienced, emphasizing the stark reality of our encounter. The question that hung heavy in the air was simple yet profound: what next?

Our adventure had taken an unexpected turn, leading us far beyond the realm of cryptozoology into the unknown territory of extraterrestrial encounters. The search for Nessie had revealed something far greater, something that could redefine our understanding of the universe. And with the first rays of dawn illuminating the Scottish Highlands, we knew our journey was going to intense. The road ahead was shrouded in mystery, but we were ready face whatever secrets the universe held for us.

The lingering hum from the alien landscape followed us as we emerged from the cave system, the metallic tang in the air a persistent reminder of our otherworldly experience. Dawn was breaking, painting the Scottish Highlands in soft pastels, a stark contrast to the vibrant, alien hues we had witnessed just hours before. We stood at the edge of the loch, the mist clinging to the surface like a shroud, the familiar landscape strangely comforting after our foray into the unknown.

Liam, ever the meticulous documentarian, was already setting up his equipment, his fingers flying across his tablet as he reviewed the footage he'd captured. The images were breathtaking, yet deeply unsettling: pulsating orbs of light, shifting geometric patterns, a spectacle that defied explanation. He muttered about needing stronger filters to reduce the glare, but even he couldn't deny the impossibility of the visuals. They were far beyond any known atmospheric phenomenon.

Ben, usually so grounded and practical, stared out at the still waters of the loch, his face etched with a mixture of wonder and unease. The geological hammer still felt alien in his hand, the metallic clang of the rocks ringing in his ears, a constant reminder of the otherworldly landscape beneath our feet. He picked up a smooth, grey stone from the bank and turned it over in his hand, tracing the patterns on the surface with a tentative finger. "I've never seen anything like it," he murmured, his voice barely audible above the gentle lapping of the water. "The rocks... they're unlike anything I've ever encountered. It's like they're... artificial."

Anya, her eyes fixed on the surface of the loch, seemed to be caught in a trance. Her temporal distortion meter still remained silent, a frustrating blankness that challenged the implications of our experience. She shifted her focus, her eyes darting towards the sky, scanning the horizon with an intensity that bordered on obsession. "The energy signatures," she whispered, her voice low and urgent, "they were unlike anything we've ever seen. They didn't just observe us; they interacted with us. The patterns were a form of communication, an attempt to bridge a chasm of understanding. But we still don't know what they wanted from us."

Eleanor, ever the pragmatist, was hunched over her laptop, her fingers flying across the keyboard. She was painstakingly analyzing the spectral data she'd collected, hoping to decipher the hidden code embedded within the light signatures. "It's a complex algorithm," she muttered, her brow furrowed in concentration. "It's like a nested language. Several different layers of information are embedded. We will need more time, more data, but this is not just random noise, this is a deliberate message. It's... staggering."

Suddenly, Anya let out a gasp, her eyes wide with a mixture of fear and awe. "Look!" she whispered, pointing towards the sky above the loch.

Above us, a single, brilliant light appeared, detaching itself from the ethereal glow of the approaching dawn. It was unlike anything we'd seen before, far brighter than the stars, pulsing with an intense, ethereal glow. It wasn't simply a point of light, but a multifaceted orb that shimmered and shifted, revealing layers of incandescent color – blues, greens, violets, all woven into a breathtaking spectacle that captivated us. The light hovered above the loch, seemingly motionless, casting an eerie, luminescent glow upon the tranquil surface of the water.

The air crackled with energy, the hum from the cave intensifying, transforming from a subtle murmur into a resonant thrum that vibrated through the very ground beneath our feet. This time, it wasn't the cold, metallic tang from the alien cave, but a warmth, a vibrant energy that seemed to emanate from the light itself, filling us with a strange mixture of awe and apprehension.

Liam's camera whirred, capturing the incredible display in stunning detail. But this time, his words were not of skepticism, but of breathless wonder. "It's... it's incredible," he whispered, his eyes glued to the viewfinder. "This is real. This isn't an illusion or a trick of the light."

Ben, forgetting his usual caution, reached out his hand, as if to touch the ethereal light. "It's beautiful," he murmured, his voice reverent. The light itself seemed to respond, pulsating gently as if in acknowledgement of his presence.

Anya, her face pale but her eyes bright with fascination, began to make frantic notes on her pad, her hand moving with a speed I'd never seen before. "The energy signature," she whispered, her voice barely audible. "It's... changing. It's more complex. This is beyond anything I've ever studied." She moved her hand towards her meter, trying to obtain a reading, but it still remained frustratingly blank, registering only a flatline.

Eleanor, ever analytical, started to record readings from her spectrometer, her brow furrowed in intense concentration. The readings were more chaotic and complex than those from the previous night, far more information-dense than before. The energy signals were interwoven with the visible light spectrum, and she was certain that some form of complex communication was occurring. It was beyond anything human technology could readily understand, but she knew instinctively that it was a message, a transmission, a bridge across the impossible divide.

The light began to move, not in erratic bursts, but with an unnerving grace, gliding above the surface of the loch as if it were floating on an invisible current. It moved slowly at first, then accelerated, becoming a blur of brilliant light that danced across the sky, weaving intricate patterns that seemed to defy the laws of physics. Then just as suddenly, as before, it vanished. It blinked out, disappearing into the dawn sky as if it had never existed.

The silence that followed was profound, almost painful. The energy, the hum, even the warmth, vanished, leaving behind a profound sense of emptiness. Yet it also left behind the indelible memory of a display more extraordinary than the night before.

We stood there for a long time, silent, staring at the peaceful surface of Loch Ness, the sun now rising fully, illuminating the familiar scenery. We had experienced something extraordinary, something that could rewrite the history of humanity itself.

Our journey hadn't ended with the discovery of the cave, nor the alien landscape. The encounter with the single light was a culmination, a proof of concept. The Loch Ness Monster, the temporal anomalies, the ancient caves, the extraterrestrial encounters—they were all connected, parts of a puzzle we were only beginning to understand. The mystery, far from being solved, had only deepened, leaving us more determined than ever to find the answers. The search for Nessie had led us to something far greater, far stranger, and far more profound than we had ever imagined. The universe was speaking to us, and we were beginning to listen. The implications were staggering, even terrifying, but we knew we couldn't ignore the call.

The lingering awe of the previous night's spectacle hung heavy in the air as we established our temporary research base. We'd chosen a secluded spot on the eastern shore of Loch Ness, far from prying eyes and shielded by a natural amphitheater of rolling hills. Liam had already erected a series of weatherproof tents, their sturdy fabric a comforting contrast to the ethereal beauty we'd witnessed. Within these temporary walls, we began the meticulous task of data collection and analysis.

Eleanor, our resident tech whiz, had already set up a sophisticated array of equipment. Her spectrometer, a marvel of engineering, hummed quietly, its sensors constantly scanning the sky, capturing even the faintest shifts in light frequencies. Next to it sat her advanced radio telescope, its parabolic dish pointed towards the heavens, listening for any faint whispers from the cosmos. Beside Eleanor's technological arsenal, Anya had positioned her temporal distortion meter, a device of her own ingenious design, capable of detecting subtle shifts in space-time. Despite its frustrating silence during the previous night's encounter, she held onto a stubborn hope that it would yield results under more controlled conditions.

Ben, our geologist, busied himself with analyzing the strange rocks he'd collected from the alien cave. He used a combination of microscopy, X-ray diffraction, and spectrographic analysis to determine their composition. The results were astonishing. The rocks contained trace elements unlike anything found on Earth, hinting at an origin far beyond our planet. Their crystalline structure, perfectly geometric and impossibly smooth, suggested a level of precision that could not have occurred naturally. Ben concluded it was artificial in origin. The more he studied them, the stronger his belief became that the cave was not merely a geological anomaly, but a manufactured structure of immense antiquity and unknown purpose.

Liam, meanwhile, spent hours meticulously reviewing the footage he'd captured of the previous night's light show. He used advanced software to enhance the images, isolating specific frequencies and analyzing the light's spectral signature. He discovered complex patterns embedded within the light, intricate geometric sequences that echoed the structure of the rocks Ben was studying. It was as if the light itself was a form of communication, a visual language we were only beginning to understand. His analysis revealed that the light's movements were not random, but deliberately choreographed, a complex dance of light and energy that seemed to follow an intricate, underlying pattern.

As the sun climbed higher, casting long shadows across the loch, Anya began to conduct her own series of experiments. She deployed a network of sensors around our base, attempting to measure the ambient electromagnetic fields. She was searching for any residual energy signatures from the previous night's encounter, any lingering echoes from the extraterrestrial display. Her readings were initially inconclusive, punctuated by bursts of unusual activity that would then disappear without explanation. However, she began to identify a pattern, a faint but persistent hum beneath the normal background noise. The hum, she surmised, was the same energy signature she'd detected during the cave exploration, and it correlated with the spectrographic analysis of the unusual rock formations.

Our days were filled with a frenetic cycle of data collection and analysis. We worked tirelessly, fueled by a mixture of adrenaline, caffeine, and a shared sense of wonder. We'd anticipated skepticism from the scientific community, but the sheer volume and complexity of the data we collected surpassed even our wildest expectations. The evidence, though circumstantial, pointed towards something extraordinary – an extraterrestrial presence, a hidden world beneath Loch Ness, and a possible connection between them, all connected somehow to Nessie.

Evenings were spent poring over the data, sharing observations, and developing theories. The contrast between the beauty and wonder of our discovery and the rigorous, analytical approach we employed was striking. We were not mere observers, but active participants in a scientific investigation of the impossible.

One evening, as we huddled around Eleanor's laptop, comparing notes, Anya let out a sharp cry. "Look at this!" she exclaimed, pointing at a complex waveform on her monitor. "The temporal distortion meter... it registered something!"

We gathered around her, our hearts pounding with a mixture of excitement and apprehension. The waveform was faint, but undeniably there—a subtle but unmistakable ripple in the fabric of space-time, coinciding with the peak of the electromagnetic hum that Anya had detected. It was a fleeting event, lasting only a fraction of a second, but it was undeniable proof that the temporal anomalies we'd experienced weren't merely figments of our imaginations. The space-time disturbances seemed directly connected to both the light shows and the energy signature detected in the rocks and from the anomalous hum.

Over the next few days, we continued our observations. We discovered that the electromagnetic hum and the temporal distortions were not random occurrences, but rather recurring phenomena, often coinciding with specific celestial events. These events, though rare, showed a correlation with periods of increased activity in the energy field, suggesting a possible extraterrestrial influence.

The most intriguing discovery came from Liam's analysis of the UFO light patterns. He discovered that the sequences were not random, but rather followed a complex mathematical formula, a language based on prime numbers and Fibonacci sequences. It seemed to be a deliberate attempt at communication, a message encoded within the visible light spectrum. It was a language beyond our current understanding, but we knew, intuitively, that it contained a message, a profound message waiting to be deciphered.

As the week wore on, our team dynamic shifted. Our initial fear and awe gave way to a focused determination. Each member embraced their unique skills and expertise, our individual strengths blending to form a unified and powerful force of investigation. We were no longer just a team; we were a collective consciousness, bound together by a shared purpose and an unyielding belief in the extraordinary. The search for Nessie had taken us on a journey into the heart of the unknown, a journey that had only just begun. The universe had spoken, and we were finally starting to listen. Our next step would involve deciphering the message from the lights, a challenge that held the key to unlocking the profound mystery at the heart of Loch Ness. The possibilities were staggering, and the potential rewards – or consequences – were immeasurable.

The rhythmic crackling of the fire provided a counterpoint to the hushed intensity of our late-night discussion. Outside, the wind whispered secrets across the still waters of Loch Ness, a constant reminder of the enigma that had brought us together. We were exhausted, running on adrenaline, a variety of not so healthy snacks and lukewarm coffee, yet the thrill of discovery kept us going. Anya, ever the optimist, traced patterns on a condensation-fogged windowpane with her finger.

"So," she began, her voice low, "we have UFOs, temporal distortions, energy signatures that defy explanation, and rocks that shouldn't exist and, of course, Nessie, the wildcard in this whole equation."

Liam, his eyes still glued to the laptop screen displaying the intricate light patterns, nodded slowly. "The light patterns are the most baffling. The mathematical sequences... they're too precise to be random. It's almost as if someone's trying to communicate with us."

Ben, ever the pragmatist, leaned forward, tapping a finger on a spread of diagrams and rock samples. "The composition of these rocks... it suggests an origin outside our solar system. But how did they get here? And what's their connection to the temporal anomalies?"

Eleanor, who had been silently analyzing data streams on her multiple monitors, chimed in, "The temporal distortions are definitely linked to the electromagnetic hum. They seem to occur in conjunction with specific celestial alignments. It's as if something is manipulating space-time itself, using the energy field as a conduit."

The swirling mist, clinging to the far shore of the loch, held me captive. My gaze was fixed on it, but my mind was miles away, wrestling with the puzzle. Silence had become my companion, a necessary cloak for the intensity of my concentration. I was piecing together the fragments, those disparate clues, feeling for the thread, the connective tissue that would finally unravel this mystery. It felt like trying to assemble a jigsaw puzzle in the dark; frustrating, exhausting, yet I couldn't stop. I had to find the solution.

"My theory," I said, my voice a little shaky, breaking the silence, "is that the Loch Ness Monster, Nessie, isn't just some creature of myth. I believe it's a key, a biological key, to unlocking something far larger, something far more profound. The cave, the UFOs, the temporal distortions... I've seen the evidence, I've pieced it together – they're all interconnected, all part of a single, vast system. Nessie, I'm convinced, is the catalyst. It's been a long road getting here, but I've reached my own conclusion."

This theory, as audacious as it was, sparked a heated debate. Liam, ever the meticulous scientist, countered, "But how? How can a creature, even an extraordinarily unique one, be the key to interdimensional travel or alien contact?"

"I considered the portholes," I countered, "the underwater openings we discovered in the loch. They aren't geological formations, I'm certain of it. They're gateways, I tell you. Nessie might be somehow attuned to these portals, capable of using them, either consciously or unconsciously, to traverse different dimensions or realities. Perhaps the UFOs are monitoring her, studying her, or even communicating with her. I believe it with all my being."

Ben added another layer to the discussion, "The rocks... their structure is almost identical to the geometric patterns in the UFO light sequences. Perhaps they're construction materials, building blocks for some kind of interdimensional infrastructure. Maybe Nessie is somehow involved in the construction or maintenance of this infrastructure."

Eleanor brought a technological perspective to the conversation, "The energy signature... it's not consistent with any known terrestrial phenomenon. It's highly organized, almost artificial in nature. It's like a cosmic hum, a background radiation that permeates this area, amplified through these unusual geological formations. And the UFOs, they seem to be interacting with this energy field, manipulating it. It could be their source of power, their propulsion system."

Anya, always one to think outside the box, added a mystical element to our analysis, "Could Nessie be a sentient being, not just an animal, but a nexus point, a bridge between our world and another? Could it be a biological antenna, receiving and transmitting signals across dimensions?"

The conversation continued late into the night, fueled by speculation, fueled by the sheer weight of our discoveries. We explored numerous possibilities, ranging from the completely rational to the wildly improbable. We considered the possibility of an ancient, technologically advanced civilization using the loch as a portal, manipulating both the environment and Nessie itself for their own purposes. We pondered the idea of a naturally occurring anomaly, a cosmic convergence of energies, perhaps a black hole or a wormhole, that was somehow linked to both Nessie and the UFO activity.

The most intriguing hypothesis involved the concept of a symbiotic relationship between Nessie and the extraterrestrial visitors. Perhaps Nessie possessed unique biological properties that the visitors found valuable, some kind of genetic material or bio-energy that was crucial to their technology or their existence. The temporal distortions could be a byproduct of this interaction, a ripple effect in the fabric of spacetime caused by the energy exchange between the two.

The idea that Nessie was not merely a relic of the past, but an active participant in ongoing extraterrestrial activity, changed our understanding of the entire situation. The monster was no longer just a mystery to be solved; it was a key to understanding a far greater enigma, a profound mystery that transcended the bounds of human comprehension.

As dawn broke, casting a pale light over the tranquil surface of the loch, we reached a tentative conclusion. While we could not definitively explain all of the phenomena we had witnessed, we were convinced that they were all linked, interconnected in ways we were only beginning to understand. Nessie was not merely a creature of legend, but a critical piece in a larger puzzle, a puzzle that extended far beyond the confines of our planet, reaching into the vast and mysterious expanse of the cosmos. Our investigation, far from being over, had only just begun. We were standing at the threshold of the unknown, and our journey into the heart of the mystery was only just starting to unfold. The next step was to delve deeper into the decipherment of the light patterns, understanding the mathematics behind this cosmic message, hoping to unlock the key to understanding the message and its potential ramifications for our world. The possibilities were endless, and the stakes were impossibly high.

The rhythmic ticking of Eleanor's chronometer punctuated the silence that followed our previous night's revelations. The fire had died down to embers, leaving only a faint warmth in the small cabin. Outside, the loch mirrored the stormy grey of the sky, a brooding presence that matched the intensity of our current task: connecting the seemingly disparate threads of our investigation.

My face, illuminated by the tablet's glow, felt hot. I traced a finger across the complex diagram, the cool glass a stark contrast to the prickle of excitement on my skin. It depicted a three-dimensional model of the cave system, a model I'd built myself, overlaid with the flight paths of the unidentified aerial phenomena we'd observed. I leaned closer, squinting. The patterns were uncanny; a shiver ran down my spine. It wasn't just a hunch anymore. The UFOs, I realized, weren't randomly traversing the skies above the loch; their movements were remarkably consistent, almost ritualistic, following precise routes that, I swear, seemed to correspond to specific points within the cave network I knew so intimately. I felt a surge of adrenaline; this was it, the breakthrough I'd been hoping for.

"Look at this," I announced, in a voice low and intense, "the primary flight paths directly correlate with the three largest chambers we found in the southern section of the cave system. It's not just proximity; it's as if they're interacting with something within those chambers."

Liam, ever the skeptic, leaned closer, his gaze scrutinizing the diagram. "Correlation doesn't equal causation, Skye. It could simply be coincidence. The loch is a vast and complex environment; it's not surprising that there's some overlap."

"But the precision, Liam," countered Ben, pointing to specific coordinates on the map. "The UFOs aren't just flying over these chambers; they're hovering, orbiting, seemingly engaging in some kind of interaction. And the energy readings from those specific locations are off the charts."

Eleanor, her eyes glued to her multiple monitors, confirmed Ben's observation. "The electromagnetic pulses are strongest in those areas. And the temporal anomalies – those subtle shifts in space-time – they're consistently clustered around the same locations. It's all converging on those three chambers."

Anya, her usual playful demeanor replaced by a focused intensity, stepped forward. "Remember the unusual rock formations we found near the entrance of the cave system? The ones with the strange geometric patterns? My analysis made sense, that their crystalline structure is incredibly similar to the energy signature emanating from the UFOs."

I nodded, picking up a small, intricately patterned rock from the table. "The patterns are identical to those we've observed in the light sequences emitted by the UFOs. It's almost as if these rocks are... components the building blocks."

The implication hung heavy in the air. The UFOs weren't just observing the loch; they were actively interacting with the cave system, using it, perhaps, for some purpose we couldn't yet fathom. And the strange rocks, with their uncanny resemblance to the UFO's light displays, suggested a possible connection to their technology or, perhaps, their very construction.

"But what's the significance of the three chambers?" Liam asked, breaking the silence.

"That's what we need to figure out," I responded, my gaze returning to the diagram. "I believe the chambers are some kind of... interface points. Points of contact between our reality and something else."

"Another dimension?" Anya whispered, her eyes wide with wonder and a touch of apprehension.

"It's a possibility," I admitted. "Remember the legends surrounding the loch, the stories of otherworldly beings and portals to different realms? These legends might not be legends at all. They could be veiled accounts of real events."

The conversation intensified, each member of the team contributing their expertise, piecing together the puzzle. Ben's geological analysis revealed that the rock formations weren't naturally occurring; their crystalline structure suggested a level of precision and complexity that defied any known geological process. Eleanor's technological insights shed light on the nature of the electromagnetic energy field, its unusually high frequency and its complex interactions with the UFOs and the cave system. Liam's meticulous scientific approach brought a necessary element of skepticism and rigor to our increasingly speculative conclusions. And Anya's intuitive insights, though unconventional, often proved surprisingly insightful, connecting disparate strands of information in unexpected ways.

Hours passed in a whirlwind of data analysis, hypothesis testing, and heated debate. We explored various possibilities, from the plausible to the utterly fantastic. Could the cave system be an ancient, alien-built structure, a kind of interdimensional gateway? Were the UFOs some kind of maintenance crew, repairing or monitoring this ancient technology? Could Nessie herself be somehow integral to this system, a biological component, or a key that unlocked the portals?

The sheer scale of the mystery was breathtaking, encompassing not only the present but the past and possibly the future. We began to understand that the Loch Ness Monster, far from being a mere anomaly, was a pivotal element within a larger, more complex system. The portholes, we realized, weren't just strange geological formations; they were the entry points, the apertures that facilitated the interaction between our world and whatever lay beyond. The UFOs weren't simply passing through; they were actively engaged, utilizing these pathways for their own purposes. And Nessie—the enigmatic creature that had captivated our imaginations—was, it seemed, deeply entwined in this interdimensional ballet.

The more we investigated, the more we realized the complexity of this enigmatic interplay between terrestrial and extraterrestrial entities. The cave system itself seemed to function as a conduit, a kind of nexus point for energy transmission and temporal distortion. The rocks, bearing an uncanny resemblance to the patterns in the UFO light displays, hinted at a sophisticated technology, perhaps even the building blocks of an interdimensional infrastructure. The energy signatures, as Eleanor had pointed out, were highly organized, exhibiting an almost artificial precision, suggesting intelligent manipulation rather than a naturally occurring phenomenon. And Nessie, the keystone of this whole intricate equation, seemed inextricably linked to it all. Was it a biological key, unlocking the secrets of these gateways? A sentient being bridging dimensions? A creature of myth, or a vital component in a far larger, cosmic process?

As the sun dipped below the horizon, casting long shadows across the loch, we found ourselves at a precipice. We had connected the dots, revealing a deeper, more complex mystery than any of us had initially imagined. But the answers remained elusive, tantalizingly out of reach. We stood at the threshold of the unknown, ready to confront a reality far beyond our wildest imaginings. The next step was clear: we had to delve deeper into the mysteries of the three chambers, to understand the nature of the interaction between the UFOs, the cave system, and the Nessie itself. The stakes were high, the unknown vast, and our quest far from over.

Chapter 4

Time Travel Theories

The fire crackled, casting dancing shadows on the faces around me. I tapped my stylus on my tablet, a complex equation shimmering on the screen. "I've been analyzing the temporal anomalies Eleanor detected," I began, my voice hushed with the weight of my revelation. "The fluctuations aren't random. They're... patterned. And I believe those patterns are linked to Nessie. It's been a long, painstaking process, pouring over the data, but I think I've finally cracked it. This could change everything." Liam raised a skeptical eyebrow. "Nessie? You're suggesting the Loch Ness Monster is somehow involved in... time travel?"

I nodded, my gaze unwavering. "Not directly, perhaps. But consider this: the cave system, the UFO activity, Nessie... they're all interconnected nodes within a larger system. A system that manipulates space-time."

I pointed to a section of my diagram, highlighting a specific area within the largest of the three chambers. "This point shows the most significant temporal distortions. It correlates directly with the strongest energy readings, and – crucially – with Nessie's observed movements. She seems to be drawn to this location, or perhaps... she's guiding something towards it. It's a feeling I've had, a sense of purpose behind her movements, almost as if she knows something I don't." Ben, ever the pragmatist, leaned forward. "What kind of 'something' are we talking about, Skye? Another UFO? Some kind of energy source?"

"I believe it's more fundamental than that," I said, my own eyes burning with what I knew was an almost feverish intensity. "I think it's a nexus point, a focal point – I've felt it, sensed it – where the fabric of space-time is thin enough to be manipulated. A kind of... natural time gate. It's something I've been working towards understanding for years, piecing together the clues, and now, I finally feel I'm close." Anya, usually quick with a joke, was unusually quiet, her eyes fixed on my tablet. "A natural time gate? That sounds... incredibly improbable."

"It is," I conceded, my voice barely a whisper. "But consider the unique geology of the region. I mean, look at the crystalline structures we found – their unusual energy signatures were unlike anything I'd ever encountered. They suggested to me a unique confluence of geological and possibly extraterrestrial forces. A naturally occurring anomaly, I reasoned, that allows for a degree of space-time manipulation. The cave system, I thought, acts as a conduit, channeling and focusing the energy. The UFOs, I suspect, are aware of this, perhaps even utilizing it for their own purposes – it's the only explanation that makes sense to me."

Eleanor, her fingers flying across her keyboard, chimed in. "The temporal anomalies are subtle, almost imperceptible to the naked eye. But my instruments are picking up minute shifts in gravitational fields, alongside the electromagnetic pulses. It's as if space-time itself is being subtly warped."

"And Nessie?" Liam pressed, his voice still laced with doubt.

"Nessie is the key, I believe," I answered, my voice firm. "She may be a biological component of this system, a living interface between our reality and... something else. A keystone of this natural time gate."

"A biological time machine?" Anya whispered, the words hanging in the air, heavy with disbelief and fascination.

I explained my theory further, drawing upon my expertise in cryptozoology and the accumulated knowledge of the team. I detailed the peculiar behavior of Nessie, its infrequent appearances, its seeming ability to disappear and reappear without a trace. Could this be more than mere elusiveness? I wondered, could it be the creature navigating shifts in space-time? The thought sent a shiver down my spine; it was a bold hypothesis, but one I felt compelled to explore.

She presented data illustrating the close correlation between Nessie's sightings and the temporal anomalies. Periods of heightened UFO activity coincided with unusual increases in reports of Nessie sightings, and the most significant temporal distortions occurred in close proximity to the creature's perceived movements. This wasn't mere coincidence, she argued, but a direct link, a symbiotic relationship between the creature, the cave system, and the extraterrestrial visitors.

"But how does it work?" Ben asked, his voice filled with a mixture of curiosity and skepticism. "What is the mechanism behind this supposed 'time gate'?"

I addressed this question carefully, walking the tightrope between scientific plausibility and outlandish speculation. I referenced the theoretical physics of wormholes and Einstein-Rosen bridges, highlighting how extreme gravitational forces could theoretically warp space-time to create tunnels through time. I suggested that the unique geological formations within the cave system, combined with the unusual energy signatures and Nessie's presence, might be creating a naturally occurring version of such a phenomenon.

"Imagine," I said, my eyes shining with excitement, "a system where the crystalline structures act as a kind of lens, focusing and amplifying the gravitational and electromagnetic forces. Nessie, with her unique biological makeup – whatever that may be – acts as a catalyst, a regulator of this energy flow, perhaps even a kind of biological conductor. The UFOs, meanwhile, may be advanced enough to understand and interact with this system, using it for their own purposes."

This wasn't a simplistic, "science fiction" interpretation. I grounded my theory in established scientific principles while acknowledging the vast unknowns. I acknowledged the significant leaps of faith my theory required. It wasn't a definitive proof but a highly plausible hypothesis, supported by the accumulated evidence. I thought that Nessie wasn't simply a creature of myth, but a vital component of a complex, naturally occurring time-travel system, accidentally discovered, possibly even manipulated by an advanced extraterrestrial civilization.

Liam remained skeptical, but the compelling nature of the evidence, the way disparate pieces of the puzzle fit together so neatly under Skye's theory, forced even him to concede the possibility. The sheer audacity of the idea – that the Loch Ness Monster might be connected to time travel – was both exhilarating and terrifying.

The discussion continued late into the night, fueled by caffeine and the sheer weight of their discovery. We debated the potential ethical implications, the risks involved in further investigation. But one thing was certain, we were no longer simply searching for a legendary monster. We were on the verge of uncovering a truth that could shake the foundations of reality itself. The quest had evolved. It was no longer just about Nessie, but about the very nature of time itself. And that made the adventure infinitely more profound and infinitely more dangerous. The next step was clear: to venture deeper into the three chambers, to get closer to the "nexus point," to understand the nature of the interaction between Nessie, the UFOs, and the potentially time-bending properties of the cave system. We all decided that it was time to go back to reality so we could figure things out.

The flickering gaslight of the Edinburgh University library cast long shadows across the ancient oak tables. I was surrounded by stacks of crumbling tomes, the musty scent of aged paper filling my nostrils.

I traced a finger across a faded map depicting the legendary Caledonian Forest. "Look at this," I murmured, my voice barely audible above the hushed whispers of other researchers. "This passage, from a 16th-century chronicle, mentions 'a beast of immense size, emerging from the mists, its scales shimmering like a thousand moons.' It places the sighting remarkably close to the location of the cave system. I felt a shiver of excitement run down my spine.

Liam, ever the skeptic, peered over my shoulder. "Anecdotal evidence at best, Skye. Legends are often embellished, exaggerated," he said, his voice laced with doubt.

"But consider the context, Liam," I countered, my eyes shining with excitement. "This account predates the modern mythologizing of Nessie. It describes physical characteristics that align with our sonar readings – the size, the scales. And the timing... I found myself leaning closer to the map, my heart pounding. The chronicle places the sighting within a period of unusually high solar activity, a period known for its electromagnetic anomalies, just as Eleanor observed near the cave system."

Anya, ever practical, chimed in, "We need more than just old legends, Skye. We need corroborating evidence. Something tangible."

I nodded. "Exactly. And that's where the Voynich manuscript comes in."

Our team shifted their focus to a digital reproduction of the Voynich manuscript – a centuries-old book filled with enigmatic illustrations and indecipherable script. Eleanor, whose expertise extended to cryptography and historical linguistics, had been studying it for weeks. "The illustrations are extraordinary," she said, her fingers tracing the contours of a bizarre creature on the screen. "This... thing... it bears a striking resemblance to Nessie, but with...modifications. Almost like a schematic, a blueprint of some kind. But that's not all. This symbol..." she pointed to a recurring pattern in the text, "...seems to correspond to specific dates within the 16th century, dates correlated with increased sightings of strange atmospheric phenomena, similar to those we've documented."

Ben, the team's geologist, leaned closer, his brow furrowed in concentration. "It's intriguing. But how do we connect these seemingly disparate events? The manuscript, the chronicle, the temporal anomalies... What's the common thread?"

I traced a finger across the timeline I'd meticulously constructed, a tapestry woven from historical accounts, astrological data, and our team's own findings. "The thread, Ben," I said, my voice low, "is time itself. These anomalies, these sightings, these cryptic manuscripts... they're not isolated incidents. I see them as echoes, ripples in the fabric of space-time, all pointing to the same underlying phenomenon: the manipulation of time. It's been a long road, piecing all this together, and I'm convinced I'm finally close to understanding it."

Our research took us to the British National Archives in Kew, a sprawling complex filled with the secrets of centuries. For days, we delved into dusty files, sifting through centuries-old reports of unexplained phenomena. They unearthed accounts of lost expeditions, vanished civilizations, and unexplained disappearances, all seemingly clustered around periods of heightened solar activity and unusual astronomical events.

One particularly intriguing document detailed the disappearance of a group of Scottish explorers in 1592, during a period known for intense displays and reports of "strange lights in the heavens." The explorers' journals, discovered decades later, contained fragmented entries hinting at an encounter with "a creature unlike any other," a creature described with unsettling accuracy to Nessie. What was even more remarkable, these journals contained cryptic symbols that mirrored those found in the Voynich manuscript.

"This is incredible," Anya breathed, her eyes wide with disbelief. "It seems every historical anomaly we look at keeps leading us back to the same place: the Loch, the caves, and that... thing."

Our research extended beyond the UK, delving into historical records from across the globe. We uncovered accounts from ancient China, detailing "sky dragons" that descended from the heavens during periods of seismic activity. From the Amazon rainforest, stories of mythical creatures emerging from hidden rivers during periods of heightened electromagnetic disturbances emerged. Even the legendary Bermuda Triangle, infamous for its disappearances, exhibited a correlation with solar flares and intense temporal anomalies according to a surprisingly comprehensive study.

Each discovery bolstered my theory, weaving together a compelling narrative that linked seemingly disparate events through a common thread – the manipulation of time and space by an unknown force. The team began to suspect that the historical records weren't simply accounts of isolated events, but fragmented glimpses into a larger, interconnected system. A system that Nessie, or something intimately connected to Nessie, was somehow controlling, or at least influenced by.

The research, far from providing simple answers, raised new, more profound questions. Was Nessie merely a creature of myth, or a key component of a naturally occurring time-travel phenomenon? Were the historical records merely embellished legends, or glimpses into real but previously unknown events, possibly caused by temporal distortions? Were the UFOs observing these events, or actively participating in them? The answers, it seemed, lay buried deep within the Earth, hidden within the very fabric of time itself.

Our team's investigation stretched far beyond the academic realm, taking them into the heart of forgotten folklore, ancient legends, and unexplored corners of human history. In the hushed halls of dusty libraries and the echoing chambers of ancient ruins, they pieced together a narrative that challenged their understanding of history, science, and the very nature of reality. The sheer audacity of their theory – that the legendary Loch Ness Monster might be the key to unlocking the secrets of time travel – was almost overwhelming. The weight of their discovery, the potential consequences of their findings, hung heavy in the air, a constant reminder of the profound and potentially dangerous path they had embarked upon. The quest to find Nessie had transformed into a race against time, a desperate chase to uncover a truth that could rewrite history itself. The stakes, they now realized, were far higher than they had ever imagined. The adventure had evolved, taking us on a journey deeper into the past, into a realm where the lines between myth and reality blurred, where the echoes of time whispered secrets that defied all known understanding. The next step – a perilous descent into the depths of the cave system – awaited them, a plunge into the heart of a mystery that threatened to shatter everything they thought they knew. So they loaded up all of their gear and headed back to the caves.

The air in the repurposed military bunker hummed with a nervous energy. Dust motes danced in the beams of high-intensity lamps, illuminating the complex array of equipment meticulously arranged across the cavernous space. This wasn't some dusty university lab; this was a high-security facility, nestled deep within the Scottish Highlands, far from prying eyes and unwanted interference. We stood around a holographic projection of the cave system beneath Loch Ness, its intricate network of tunnels shimmering in three dimensions.

"Right," I said, my voice clear and steady despite the palpable tension. "The plan is threefold. First, we need to establish a baseline. Eleanor, you'll be monitoring the electromagnetic fluctuations within and around the cave system. We need a precise record of the ambient energy levels before we introduce any variables."

Eleanor, her fingers flying across a complex console, nodded. "Already monitoring, Skye. Background radiation is stable, within expected parameters. But there are...subtle anomalies. Minor fluctuations, barely detectable, but consistent. It's as if something is...pulsating beneath the surface."

"Exactly," I said, "That pulsing, those subtle fluctuations... that's the key. That's what we believe is causing the temporal distortions."

"And the second phase?" Ben asked, his gaze fixed on the holographic map. He'd been instrumental in designing and constructing the specialized equipment for their experiment, a blend of cutting-edge technology and salvaged components from decommissioned military projects.

"Phase two involves the chronometer," I explained, gesturing towards a large, cylindrical device humming softly in the corner. "Ben's masterpiece. It's designed to measure even the slightest shifts in temporal flow. We'll place it at the cave entrance, and at several key points deeper within the system. The readings should provide irrefutable evidence of time distortions, if they exist."

Ben adjusted a series of dials on the chronometer, his movements precise and confident. "The chronometer is highly sensitive. It can detect variations in time down to fractions of a second. But even the slightest environmental interference can throw it off."

"And that's where the third phase comes in," Anya said, her voice firm and measured. "We need to trigger the time distortion artificially, if possible. We hypothesize that the electromagnetic fields created by the unusual rock formations within the cave system, in combination with the heightened solar activity we've observed, are crucial. We'll utilize a modified Tesla coil to generate a focused electromagnetic pulse, mimicking the conditions observed during past anomalies."

Liam, still the skeptic, voiced his concerns. "This is incredibly risky, Skye. We're talking about manipulating the fabric of space-time. We have no idea what the consequences might be. A minor miscalculation could..."

"Could cause a paradox, temporal displacement, or a rip in space-time," I finished for him, my voice calm but firm. "Yes, Liam, we know the risks. That's why we're taking every precaution. The bunker is shielded, the equipment is fail-safe, and we have contingency plans in place."

"But what about the ethical implications?" Liam pressed, his gaze troubled. "What if we inadvertently alter the past or the future?"

I met his gaze directly. "Liam, we're not playing God here. We're scientists, researchers. We're seeking to understand, not to control. If we can prove that time travel is possible, the ethical ramifications are far-reaching, but we'll face those challenges as they arise. For now, we must proceed with our experiment."

We meticulously prepared for the experiment, a delicate dance between scientific precision and the inherent unpredictability of time travel. Anya calibrated the modified Tesla coil, its intricate wiring a testament to her engineering prowess. Ben ran diagnostics on the chronometer, ensuring its sensitivity and accuracy. Eleanor meticulously checked her electromagnetic sensors, ensuring their readiness to capture any significant fluctuation. Liam, though still hesitant, meticulously documented every step of the process. I, the driving force behind the project, oversaw the entire operation, my eyes filled with a mixture of hope and trepidation.

The countdown began, the tension in the bunker palpable. Five... four... three... two... one... Anya activated the Tesla coil, a surge of energy coursing through the device, creating a localized electromagnetic field that pulsed and shimmered within the confined space. The bunker vibrated slightly, and the air crackled with energy.

The chronometer registered an immediate shift, the numbers on its digital display fluctuating wildly. Eleanor's sensors began to register unusual electromagnetic activity, readings far beyond anything they had observed previously. A low hum filled the bunker, growing in intensity, accompanied by an unnerving silence that seemed to amplify the sounds of our own heartbeats. The holographic projection of the cave system flickered, distorting and shifting before their eyes.

Then, as suddenly as it began, the energy surge subsided. The hum faded, the silence returning to a normal level, and I watched the holographic projection stabilize. I held my breath, my mind racing to interpret the data. The chronometer readings were staggering, indicating a minute but measurable time dilation – a confirmation, however small, that our experiment had indeed affected the flow of time. I felt a jolt of exhilaration, mixed with a healthy dose of disbelief. Could it really be? We had done it.

The analysis of the data was painstaking. Days were spent scrutinizing the readings from the chronometer, comparing them against Eleanor's electromagnetic recordings. Ben meticulously cross-referenced the data with historical records, searching for correlations between the temporal distortions and the accounts of historical anomalies. Anya ran simulations, modeling the effects of the electromagnetic pulse on the cave system. Liam, finally relinquishing some of his skepticism, helped to compile the data and offer insightful perspectives.

Our findings were nothing short of revolutionary. The experiment had not only confirmed the existence of temporal distortions linked to the cave system but also provided compelling evidence of the manipulation of time. The data suggested that the cave system itself was a kind of natural time portal, its activity amplified by specific electromagnetic conditions.

However, the data also raised new, more complex questions. The subtle changes in temporal flow detected by the chronometer indicated that the distortions were far more intricate than we had initially imagined. The precise mechanism behind the time manipulation remained a mystery. And the potential consequences of further experimentation remained profoundly unclear.

The implications of their discovery were staggering. The quest to understand the Loch Ness Monster had inadvertently led us to the edge of a scientific revolution. The line between myth and reality had blurred beyond recognition. And the path ahead, now that they'd glimpsed the possibility of controlling time itself, was shrouded in both immense potential and considerable peril. The adventure, it seemed, was far from over. Our next steps would require even greater caution, greater precision, and a far deeper understanding of the forces we had awakened. The whispers of time had revealed a truth more profound, more terrifying, and more exhilarating than any we could have imagined.

The silence following the cessation of the electromagnetic pulse hung heavy in the air, thick with unspoken anticipation. The chronometer, instead of settling back to its baseline reading, continued to fluctuate, its digital display a chaotic dance of numbers. Eleanor's sensors shrieked, emitting a cacophony of alarms that pierced the previous quietude. The holographic projection of the cave system pulsed erratically, its shimmering lines distorting into grotesque shapes before abruptly vanishing altogether.

"What's happening?" Liam's voice, usually steady, cracked with a hint of panic. He stared at the empty space where the three-dimensional map had been, his face a mask of disbelief.

My gaze was glued to the chronometer's wildly fluctuating readings, a cold dread seizing my heart. This wasn't the subtle time dilation we'd anticipated; this was something far more significant, far more dangerous. The minor fluctuations we'd initially observed had escalated into a full-blown temporal anomaly. I felt a prickle of fear, a cold sweat breaking out on my skin. This was beyond anything I'd ever experienced, beyond anything I'd ever imagined. My breath hitched in my throat. What was happening? What had we done?

"The pulse... it didn't just create a localized distortion," Anya breathed, her fingers dancing across her console, trying to make sense of the overwhelming data flooding in. "It seems to have...amplified something already present. Something far larger, far more powerful."

Ben, his brow furrowed in concentration, leaned over the chronometer, his fingers tracing the erratic patterns on its display. "The time dilation... it's accelerating. It's not just a shift; it's a cascading effect. We're seeing multiple temporal displacements, overlapping, interacting...it's like...a ripple effect in a pond, only instead of water, it's time."

A low hum, far deeper and more resonant than the one produced by the Tesla coil, filled the bunker. The air grew cold, a chill that seeped into their bones despite the warmth of the equipment surrounding us. The lights flickered, casting long, dancing shadows that seemed to writhe and twist before our eyes.

Suddenly, a shimmering distortion appeared in the air, a tear in the fabric of reality itself. From within it, a swirling vortex of light and color emerged, pulsating with an otherworldly energy. The vortex expanded rapidly, consuming a significant portion of the bunker's space.

Panic threatened to overwhelm us. Liam stumbled backward, his eyes wide with terror. Anya gasped, her hands flying over her console in a desperate attempt to regain control. Ben remained rooted to the spot, his gaze fixated on the expanding vortex, a mixture of awe and fear etched on his face. Eleanor, her face pale, continued to monitor the sensors, her fingers flying across the keyboard, seemingly oblivious to the unfolding chaos.

I, however, felt a strange calmness settle over me. Years of studying the unexplained, of confronting the unknown, had prepared me for moments like this. This wasn't just a scientific experiment gone wrong; this was a portal, a gateway to another time, another reality. And I, along with my team, was about to step through it.

"Everyone, stay calm!" I shouted, "This is… unexpected, but we can manage this. Ben, assess the stability of the vortex. Anya, try to isolate the source of the temporal anomaly. Eleanor, continue monitoring the energy readings. Liam, document everything!"

My team, spurred into action by my command, worked with a frantic efficiency. Ben used his specialized equipment to analyze the vortex, his calculations appearing on a nearby screen as fast as he could perform them. Anya fought against the overwhelming data pouring from her sensors, attempting to unravel the complex pattern of the temporal displacement. Eleanor's readings showed energy levels surpassing anything previously recorded; the numbers were off the scale. Liam, despite his terror, managed to keep his notes up-to-date, chronicling each step of this chaotic event.

The vortex pulsed and shifted, growing larger, its energy intensifying. It began to emit a low, guttural sound, a sound that resonated deep within their chests, vibrating their very bones.

"It's pulling us in," Eleanor whispered, her eyes fixed on the ever-expanding anomaly.

The temporal distortion affected not only time, but also space. Objects around the bunker began to shimmer and distort, their forms wavering like heat haze on a summer day. The air itself seemed to vibrate, causing a disorienting wave of nausea. The ground beneath our feet felt unstable, as if the bunker itself was being pulled into the vortex.

Suddenly, a figure emerged from the swirling vortex. It was tall, humanoid, but its features were obscured by the shimmering light. It wore clothes that seemed both ancient and futuristic, a paradox of textures and styles that defied explanation. Its eyes, however, were clearly visible, glowing with an eerie luminescence.

The figure raised a hand, and the vortex pulsed violently, growing still larger. The air crackled with energy, and a wave of dizziness washed over us. Then, as abruptly as it had appeared, the figure vanished back into the vortex, leaving us standing in stunned silence.

The immediate crisis had passed, but a new, more profound fear had settled upon us. The experiment had not only opened a gateway to another time but had also revealed the existence of beings from that time, beings whose intentions were completely unknown.

The chronometer's readings continued to fluctuate wildly, the energy levels remained dangerously high, and the potential for further temporal distortions loomed large. Their initial quest to understand the Loch Ness Monster had led them to something far more significant, something far more perilous. The mystery of Nessie remained unsolved, yet now a far greater mystery—the mystery of time travel, and the beings that controlled it—lay before us, demanding answers. The unexpected consequences of their experiment had opened a Pandora's Box of possibilities. We had glimpsed a future, or perhaps a past, that was both terrifying and utterly compelling. We knew, with certainty, that their journey into the heart of this enigma was far from over. The world, and perhaps even time itself, had irrevocably changed.

The air crackled with an energy that was both terrifying and exhilarating. The vortex, no longer a simple swirling mass of light, had solidified, its edges sharpening into a defined, shimmering oval. Within its depths, images flickered – fleeting glimpses of landscapes both familiar and utterly alien. Jagged peaks pierced a sky ablaze with an unfamiliar constellation; lush, primeval forests teemed with creatures that defied categorization; colossal structures of impossible geometry rose from the earth, their surfaces etched with symbols that resembled nothing I had ever encountered.

Then, as abruptly as the images appeared, they vanished, replaced by a kaleidoscopic explosion of color and light. The hum intensified, morphing into a resonant chord that resonated deep within our bones, a vibration that seemed to shake our very souls. The ground trembled, the bunker groaning under the strain of the immense temporal forces at play.

And then, the world changed.

One moment, we were in their secure, technologically advanced bunker, the next we stood on a beach bathed in the crimson glow of a double sunset. The air hung heavy with the scent of salt and decaying vegetation, a primal, almost suffocating aroma. The sand beneath our feet was coarse and black, speckled with iridescent shells that resembled nothing found in the present day. Above, the sky pulsed with the strange, ethereal glow of two suns, casting long, distorted shadows that stretched and warped across the alien landscape.

The technology surrounding us – the chronometer, the sensors, the holographic projectors – had vanished, replaced by a primitive, almost terrifying silence. The only sound was the rhythmic crash of waves against the shore, a relentless percussion that echoed the pounding in our hearts.

Liam, his face a mask of pale terror, stumbled back, his eyes wide with disbelief. He reached out a trembling hand to touch the black sand, his fingers retracting quickly as if burned. "What... what happened?" he stammered, his voice barely a whisper.

Anya, her usually sharp intellect momentarily overwhelmed, stared around with a dazed expression. "The temporal displacement... it wasn't just a glimpse. We're... we're here. In another time."

Ben, ever the pragmatist, began a methodical examination of their surroundings. He knelt, carefully examining the strange shells scattered across the beach. "The composition... it's unlike anything I've ever seen. The isotopes are... shifted. This isn't just a different location; it's a different era."

Eleanor, her face pale but her eyes gleaming with scientific curiosity, began recording data with a small, hand-held device that seemed to have materialized from thin air. She murmured to herself, her fingers flying across its intricate keypad, as if trying to make sense of this unbelievable reality.

I, despite the chaos, felt a strange sense of calm. The years of research, the countless hours spent studying anomalies, had prepared me for the unimaginable. This wasn't merely a scientific curiosity; it was a journey into the heart of history, a plunge into the unknown.

"We need to assess our situation," I said, my voice firm despite the tremor in my hands. "Ben, analyze the environment. Anya, try to establish communication – if possible. Eleanor, continue documenting everything. Liam, stay alert."

Ben's analysis revealed a staggering truth. The air was breathable, but the composition was significantly different, with higher levels of certain gases that suggested a less oxygen-rich atmosphere. The plants were alien, exhibiting bioluminescent properties that cast a soft, eerie glow upon the landscape. The strange shells, upon closer examination, contained microscopic organisms unlike any known to science.

Anya's attempts at communication yielded nothing. There were no radio signals, no electronic interference – only silence. The past, it seemed, was devoid of the technological noise of the present.

As dusk descended, the twin suns painted the sky in hues of blood orange and deep violet. Giant, fern-like plants unfurled their bioluminescent leaves, illuminating the landscape with an ethereal, otherworldly glow. Strange, reptilian sounds echoed through the twilight, adding to the unsettling atmosphere.

We found shelter in a natural cave formed within a cliff face, its entrance partially concealed by a thick curtain of vegetation. Inside, we huddled together, the darkness punctuated only by Eleanor's device and the soft glow of the bioluminescent flora outside. The air within the cave was humid and damp, carrying the scent of decaying organic matter and the faint, metallic tang of blood.

The night brought a chilling revelation. Giant, winged creatures, their forms indistinct in the twilight, descended from the sky, their silhouettes resembling monstrous bats. They circled the cave, their eerie cries echoing across the primeval landscape. Their movements were predatory, swift and silent, and a primal fear tightened its grip on us.

As dawn approached, painting the sky in muted shades of grey and purple, the winged creatures vanished. We emerged from the cave, our hearts pounding, still reeling from the events of the night. We realized with sobering clarity that our time travel experiment had taken us to a time far more perilous than we could have ever imagined. This was a world where the laws of nature were different, where survival depended on adapting to an environment hostile and unforgiving.

We continued our exploration, carefully navigating the unfamiliar terrain. We encountered strange flora and fauna, witnessing ecosystems unlike anything seen in the modern world. We found evidence of a civilization, ruins of colossal structures suggesting a society far advanced for its time, yet mysteriously vanished. The symbols we discovered on the ruins mirrored the images we had glimpsed within the vortex, fueling our belief that the civilization had some connection to the temporal anomaly.

Our journey wasn't just a journey through time, but a plunge into the heart of a mystery that echoed from the dawn of time. Loch Ness, initially my obsession, became a trivial footnote to the profound enigma we'd stumbled upon. I was no longer just a cryptozoologist hunting a myth; I was an explorer of time, a witness to a lost world, an unwitting participant in a historical puzzle that could rewrite everything I thought I knew about the past – and perhaps, the future. The temporal rift hadn't just opened a gateway to another time; it opened a gateway to understanding the very nature of time itself. This journey would test my limits, my courage, and my sanity. I felt a thrill, a terror, and a profound sense of wonder all at once. My heart pounded with the immensity of what we'd discovered.

Chapter 5

Confronting Skeptics

The discovery of the prehistoric beach, the alien flora and fauna, and the unsettling encounters with the nocturnal winged creatures didn't stay hidden for long. News of their extraordinary expedition leaked, initially through hushed whispers in scientific circles, then exploding into a full blown media frenzy. The initial reports were cautious, tentative, filled with phrases like "unsubstantiated claims" and "alleged temporal displacement." But as more details emerged—grainy photographs of the bizarre landscape, fragmented video footage of the bioluminescent flora, and even blurry images of the massive winged creatures—the story ignited the public imagination.

The internet exploded. Blogs, forums, and social media platforms were flooded with speculation, conspiracy theories, and outright ridicule. Nessie TimeTravel became a trending hashtag, a bizarre confluence of cryptozoology, science fiction, and historical speculation. Some hailed the team as pioneers, brave explorers pushing the boundaries of human understanding; others dismissed them as delusional, attention-seeking charlatans.

My team found themselves at the center of a maelstrom. Our every move was scrutinized, our words dissected, our credibility constantly under attack. The initial euphoria of our discovery quickly morphed into a relentless barrage of criticism and doubt. Reputable news outlets reached out for interviews, eager to capitalize on the sensational story, but the pressure was immense. Each interview felt like a tightrope walk, a delicate balance between conveying the awe-inspiring nature of their findings and avoiding accusations of fabrication or scientific incompetence.

One particularly aggressive journalist, a notorious skeptic with a penchant for debunking paranormal phenomena, became our chief antagonist. He relentlessly pursued us, bombarding us with skeptical questions, demanding irrefutable proof, and twisting our words to create sensationalist headlines that undermined our credibility. His articles were loaded with condescending tones, his arguments carefully crafted to exploit any perceived weakness in their narrative.

Public forums became battlegrounds. Online discussions descended into chaotic arguments, with supporters and detractors clashing vehemently. Conspiracy theories flourished, some suggesting that the entire expedition was a sophisticated hoax, others claiming it was a government cover-up designed to obscure a far more significant discovery. The pressure mounted on me, impacting my ability to focus on the scientific analysis of our findings. Sleepless nights were spent responding to emails, conducting interviews, and trying to maintain some semblance of control amidst the chaos.

The scientific community was equally divided. Some respected academics cautiously acknowledged the potential significance of their discovery, urging further investigation and a rigorous analysis of the data. Others, entrenched in traditional scientific paradigms, dismissed their claims as pseudoscience, highlighting gaps in their evidence and questioning the reliability of their methods. We faced accusations of reckless experimentation, of disregarding established scientific protocols, and of jeopardizing the integrity of scientific research.

A series of televised debates further fueled the controversy. My team and I found ourselves pitted against prominent skeptics, forced to defend our findings against relentless questioning and often deliberately misleading arguments. I felt the pressure mounting with each aggressive line of questioning. The format, designed to generate conflict rather than promote rational discourse, only served to amplify the already intense polarization. I could see the frustration building in my colleagues' faces as well. The public, caught in the crossfire, was left unsure of whom to believe—and I understood their confusion. The stakes were incredibly high: not only were our reputations on the line, but the very possibility of the acceptance of time travel as a legitimate scientific concept hung in the balance. I felt the weight of that responsibility heavily on my shoulders.

Liam, already prone to anxiety, struggled to cope with the intense media scrutiny. He withdrew from the public eye, focusing instead on analyzing the samples collected from the prehistoric beach, hoping that the scientific data could provide irrefutable proof of their experience. He worked tirelessly in his lab, analyzing the unique isotopes, the unusual microorganisms, the strange mineral compositions, but the media frenzy only seemed to amplify his fear of failure.

Anya, ever the strategist, was determined to manage the public perception of their findings. She worked closely with a public relations firm, carefully crafting press releases, organizing controlled interviews, and managing the team's online presence. But even her sharp intellect and strategic skills seemed inadequate to quell the tide of skepticism and outright hostility.

Ben, ever the pragmatist, focused on the practical aspects of their predicament. He diligently documented every piece of evidence, meticulously cataloging every observation, carefully organizing the data they'd gathered. He sought expert opinions from specialists in various fields, striving to bolster their claims with corroborative data from independent sources. However, even his meticulous work couldn't completely silence the chorus of doubt and criticism.

Eleanor, though usually reserved, became a surprising advocate. She skillfully navigated the complexities of scientific discourse, responding to criticisms with reasoned arguments and providing scientific context to their findings. She became a strong voice in the scientific community, defending her colleagues and meticulously refuting misleading accusations. Her composure and reasoned approach gained respect, even from some of the most ardent skeptics.

I felt the weight of it all acutely. The years of research, the risks we had taken, the extraordinary journey we had undertaken—all seemed threatened by the relentless barrage of doubt and skepticism. I recognized that our adventure wasn't just about proving our theories about Nessie or time travel; it was about confronting the inherent limitations of human understanding, the challenges of confronting established paradigms, and the burden of carrying the truth against an ocean of prejudice and misunderstanding. The battle was far from over; the true test of our discovery wasn't just proving its validity, but in navigating the complex social and political landscape surrounding scientific innovation. The media frenzy felt like a battlefield, and I knew that only through reasoned argument, scientific rigor, and unwavering determination could we hope to win the war. The fate of our discovery, and perhaps the future of scientific progress itself, hung in the balance. I felt the pressure intensely; the responsibility was immense.

The first televised debate felt like a trial by fire. My heart hammered against my ribs as I sat on that starkly lit stage, flanked by my team. Sweat beaded on my forehead despite the air conditioning. I could feel the eyes of the panel – those renowned skeptics – boring into me. Each one a seasoned veteran, ready to tear apart any weakness in my argument. The moderator, a silver-haired veteran journalist known for his unflinching interrogation style, introduced the topic with a theatrical flourish: "Tonight, we examine the extraordinary claims of the MacDougall expedition – claims that defy logic, challenge established science, and border on the fantastical. Are these intrepid explorers pioneers of a new era of discovery, or simply purveyors of a sophisticated hoax?" I swallowed hard, my throat suddenly dry. This was it. Everything I had worked for, everything we had risked rested on this moment.

The air crackled with anticipation. The lead skeptic, Dr. Alistair Finch, a renowned physicist with a reputation for dismantling pseudoscientific claims, launched into a scathing critique. "Your evidence, Ms. MacDougall, is anecdotal at best. Blurry photographs, grainy video footage, unsubstantiated eyewitness accounts – these are hardly the cornerstones of scientific rigor. Where's the concrete evidence? The irrefutable proof?"

I kept my voice steady, though my insides were a whirlwind of nerves. "Dr. Finch," I said calmly, "we understand the need for rigorous scientific evidence. We've already published our initial findings in peer-reviewed journals, including detailed geological surveys, isotopic analysis of the prehistoric beach samples, and botanical analysis of the alien flora. These papers, while challenging existing paradigms, are based on meticulously documented data."

I gestured towards Ben. He leaned forward, projecting a slide showcasing the geological cross-section of the cave system leading to the prehistoric beach. "Ben's geological analysis," I continued, "reveals a unique geological formation unlike anything known in this region. I saw it myself in the strata – evidence of rapid deposition, and the presence of minerals I'd never encountered in this geographical area."

Ben added, his voice measured and confident, "The isotopic dating of the sediment samples, independently verified by three separate labs, confirms their prehistoric origin. The age of the samples aligns with the time period indicated by the temporal displacement events."

Eleanor then took the floor, explaining the unique characteristics of the discovered flora. "The biochemical analysis of the alien plants reveals cellular structures and metabolic processes entirely unlike any known terrestrial species. Their bioluminescence, as documented in multiple high-resolution photographs and video footage, is another anomaly that defies conventional botanical understanding."

Anya chimed in, showing a series of maps and satellite imagery. "Furthermore, our research into the unexplained UFO activity corresponds to the temporal displacement events. The satellite imagery shows unusual energy signatures near the cave system during the periods when we experienced the temporal shifts. This correlation suggests a potential link between the phenomena."

Liam, usually reticent, spoke up, his voice laced with quiet intensity. "The microbial analysis of the samples from the prehistoric beach revealed unique microorganisms with DNA sequences unlike anything in our existing databases. These organisms exhibit remarkable resilience to extreme environmental conditions, hinting at possible adaptations beyond our current understanding."

Dr. Finch, however, remained unconvinced. He countered with a barrage of pointed questions, challenging the validity of their dating methods, questioning the reliability of their sampling techniques, and highlighting inconsistencies in their narratives. The debate became a fierce intellectual battle, a clash of evidence and skepticism, a testing ground for the strength of their scientific arguments and the depth of their belief in their discoveries.

The subsequent press conference was equally challenging. Journalists, armed with pre-prepared, pointed questions, pressed us relentlessly. Accusations of fabrication, conspiracy theories, and suggestions of a carefully orchestrated hoax were thrown at us from all sides. I felt the heat of the spotlights, the weight of their skepticism pressing down. But I remained composed. I explained our research methodology in detail, emphasizing the rigorous scientific protocols we had followed. I showed them the independent verification of our data, highlighted the collaborative nature of our research, and pointed to the meticulous documentation of our expedition. I knew we'd done everything by the book, and I was determined to convey that. The pressure was immense, but I held my ground, answering each question as clearly and precisely as I could.

Anya expertly managed the media narrative, directing the conversation toward the more scientifically compelling aspects of their findings. She presented compelling evidence of the prehistoric beach, the unique flora and fauna, and the anomalous energy readings. Ben, with his meticulous documentation, provided precise answers to technical questions, reassuring the audience of the scientific rigor of their work. Liam focused on the implications of the unique microbial life forms, emphasizing the potential for groundbreaking scientific discoveries. Eleanor deftly countered the accusations of scientific misconduct and defended their methods with a well-reasoned approach.

The publication of their findings in several reputable scientific journals marked a pivotal moment. While skepticism remained, the detailed data, the independent verifications, and the rigorous analysis began to shift the balance. The papers sparked a wave of further research, with scientists from various disciplines examining their data, attempting to replicate our findings, and exploring the implications of our work.

The fight was far from over, the battle for acceptance a protracted war of attrition. Yet, with each meticulously documented fact, each independently verified data point, each reasoned argument, the team steadily chipped away at the wall of skepticism. Their journey was a testament to the perseverance of scientific inquiry, the importance of challenging existing paradigms, and the enduring power of truth in the face of doubt. The Loch Ness Monster, whether or not it truly existed in the traditional sense, had become a catalyst for a far greater and more profound revelation, a doorway to an understanding of reality that challenged the very limits of human perception and comprehension. The unfolding story was not only about Nessie, but about the incredible journey of scientific discovery itself. The journey, which was fraught with dangers, uncertainty and skepticism, was proving to be a compelling story of human endeavor, echoing through scientific forums, university seminars and even reaching the front pages of the leading global news outlets. Our team had won a battle, but the war for acceptance had only just begun. The truth, once hidden deep beneath the waters of the loch, was now slowly rising to the surface.

The publication of our findings in Nature and Science didn't magically silence the skeptics; it merely shifted the battlefield. I remember the initial wave of articles – while acknowledging the meticulous nature of our research, they were cautiously worded, often focusing on the "anomalies" rather than the revolutionary implications. I felt the familiar sting of scientific hesitancy; the community, a bastion of rigorous methodology and peer review, was predictably reluctant to embrace conclusions that overturned established paradigms.

The first major academic conference following the publication became a crucible for intense debate. I stood in the lecture hall, and saw sea of faces illuminated by the flickering projector light showcasing Ben's geological cross-sections, and felt a knot of anxiety tighten in my stomach. I, though now accustomed to the pressure of public scrutiny, presented our findings with a confident authority that belied her initial apprehension – an apprehension I shared. I watched as she meticulously laid bare the layers of evidence we had amassed: the anomalous geological formations, the isotopic dating of the prehistoric beach, the unique flora and fauna. The presentation sparked a heated exchange.

Then, Dr. Anya Sharma, a leading astrophysicist, stepped forward. I leaned forward, captivated, as she addressed the most challenging aspect of our findings: the temporal displacements. Her complex mathematical model, supported by data from the satellite imagery and the energy readings, suggested a localized distortion of space-time near the cave system. I remember thinking, this could actually work, as she presented her theory, a mechanism by which the temporal anomalies could have occurred, linking them to the unique geological and biological phenomena we'd identified Her explanation, however, was met with immediate counterarguments from several physicists who questioned her model's viability, suggesting alternative explanations for the energy signatures and dismissing the temporal displacement data as flawed or misinterpreted.

The subsequent question-and-answer session was a whirlwind. I found myself fielding questions about the dating techniques, defending our methodology with detailed explanations of the various isotopic ratios and the independent verification of our results. It was exhausting, but exhilarating. I heard Liam, usually reserved, speak with newfound confidence, explaining the unique adaptations of the microorganisms and the potential implications for understanding extremophile life. I watched Eleanor address the botanical anomalies, showcasing the detailed biochemical analysis and defending her interpretations against skepticism. It felt like a battle, but we fought with the weight of our evidence behind us.

One particularly vocal critic, Dr. Evelyn Reed, a renowned paleontologist, challenged the interpretation of the fossil evidence, suggesting alternative explanations for the rapid deposition of the sediment layers and questioning the uniqueness of the discovered flora. Her argument hinged on the possibility of previously unknown geological processes or the misidentification of the plant species. The ensuing debate between Dr. Reed and Eleanor escalated into a passionate exchange of scientific evidence and interpretations, highlighting the inherent uncertainties and complexities of scientific inquiry.

The debate extended beyond the confines of the conference hall. Articles in scientific journals were meticulously dissected, each data point scrutinized, each interpretation challenged. The initial excitement and curiosity gave way to a more rigorous assessment, a thorough examination of the evidence, and a careful evaluation of the implications. Some scientists lauded the MacDougall team's work as groundbreaking, a paradigm shift in our understanding of geology, biology, and even physics. Others remained steadfast in their skepticism, highlighting the need for further research and independent verification. Reputable scientific journals published counterarguments, critiques, and reinterpretations of the team's data, contributing to a complex and multifaceted scientific debate.

The subsequent months saw a flurry of replications, verifications, and further research initiatives. Scientists from various disciplines, inspired by the MacDougall team's work, embarked on their own investigations, attempting to replicate their findings, and explore the implications of their work. New data emerged, some supporting the MacDougall team's findings, others challenging our interpretations. The initial excitement and controversy surrounding the our discovery slowly gave way to a more nuanced and methodical approach, a testament to the scientific process of rigorous inquiry, peer review, and relentless pursuit of knowledge.

The journey through the labyrinth of scientific debate was far from easy. We faced constant pressure, our findings scrutinized from every angle, our credibility repeatedly questioned. However, we steadfastly adhered to the principles of scientific rigor, documenting every step of our research, providing detailed explanations of our methodologies, and submitting our findings to the scrutiny of the scientific community. I remember the sleepless nights, the endless revisions, and the doubt that crept into my thoughts sometimes.

The debate, however, wasn't solely confined to academic circles. I saw firsthand how the public, captivated by the narrative of the Loch Ness Monster, followed our unfolding story with intense interest.

News articles, documentaries, and even fictionalized accounts of our expedition fueled public imagination and debate. This public interest, while sometimes fueled by sensationalism, also ensured continued scrutiny and encouraged further investigation. The pressure was immense, but I felt a growing sense of responsibility, knowing that our work was under constant observation.

Eventually, the weight of evidence began to tip the scales. It was incredibly satisfying to see independent researchers replicate our key findings, verifying the existence of the unique flora and fauna, confirming the age of the prehistoric beach, and supporting the anomalies we'd detected in the geological formations. While complete acceptance of the temporal displacement theory remained elusive, I could feel the shift in the scientific community – a growing acknowledgement of the potential for a radical re-evaluation of our understanding of the natural world. It was a culmination of years of relentless work, and a profound moment for me personally.

Our team's journey became a compelling case study in the evolution of scientific knowledge, a testament to the resilience of scientific inquiry, and a powerful example of how revolutionary discoveries can emerge from seemingly implausible beginnings. The initial skepticism, while understandable and even necessary, eventually yielded to the weight of meticulously gathered evidence and rigorous scientific analysis. The battle was not over, but the tide was slowly turning in their favor. The truth, once obscured by the murky depths of Loch Ness, was finally beginning to emerge into the light of scientific acceptance. The long journey to uncover the secrets of Nessie had also inadvertently unveiled a far greater mystery, one that pushed the boundaries of scientific understanding and challenged humanity's perception of reality itself.

The relentless scrutiny continued, a tidal wave of peer reviews, replications, and counter-arguments crashing over our team. Each published paper felt like a gauntlet thrown down, a challenge to defend our findings against the sharpest minds in their respective fields. The initial euphoria of publication in Nature and Science had faded, replaced by the grinding work of solidifying their position, reinforcing their arguments, and anticipating the inevitable counterattacks.

Ben, ever the pragmatist, focused on bolstering the geological evidence. He organized a second, independent geological survey of the area, inviting prominent skeptics to participate. This wasn't a mere gesture of goodwill; it was a calculated strategy. By including Dr. Reed, the paleontologist who had vehemently challenged their initial interpretation of the sediment layers, Ben ensured a truly independent assessment. The results, painstakingly compiled and meticulously documented, largely corroborated their initial findings. While some nuances differed, the overall picture remained consistent: the geological formations were anomalous, hinting at processes previously unknown to science. The inclusion of Dr. Reed's signature on the subsequent joint publication was a symbolic victory, a testament to the power of unbiased investigation.

Eleanor, meanwhile, delved deeper into the botanical mysteries. The unique flora, with its peculiar bioluminescent properties and strange genetic makeup, demanded further investigation. She collaborated with a team of geneticists and botanists from the University of Edinburgh, conducting extensive genomic sequencing and phylogenetic analysis. Our research not only confirmed the uniqueness of the plants but also hinted at an evolutionary pathway drastically different from anything previously observed. This groundbreaking discovery, published in

Proceedings of the Royal Society B, further strengthened the credibility of the MacDougall team's findings, shifting the focus from isolated anomalies to a broader, more compelling pattern of evidence.

Liam, initially reticent to step into the spotlight, found his voice amplified by the weight of the data. His research on the extremophile microorganisms, their resilience to extreme conditions, and their surprisingly complex symbiotic relationships, gained traction among microbiologists and astrobiologists alike. His findings held significant implications for the understanding of life's origins and its capacity to thrive in seemingly impossible environments. The publication of his findings in a respected astrobiology journal resonated beyond the scientific community, capturing the imagination of a wider audience interested in the potential for extraterrestrial life.

I was the driving force behind the entire project, orchestrating a series of public lectures and interviews. I abandoned the rigid academic language of scientific papers, opting for a more accessible, engaging style. I explained the complexities of my research in simple terms, weaving the scientific details into a captivating narrative. This approach resonated with the public, dispelling much of the initial apprehension surrounding the unconventional nature of our discoveries. I deftly used the platform to not only present the evidence but to also showcase the meticulous research process, highlighting the scientific method's strength in challenging assumptions and biases. My charismatic presentation style, combined with the undeniable weight of the scientific data, began to turn the tide of public opinion.

The controversy, however, didn't entirely disappear. The temporal anomalies remained the most contentious point. While Dr. Sharma's theoretical model offered a plausible explanation, the lack of concrete proof continued to fuel skepticism. Our team acknowledged the limitations of their data, emphasizing the need for further research to solidify this aspect of their findings. We openly discussed the uncertainties and the potential for alternative explanations, fostering a climate of open debate and collaborative inquiry rather than defensive posturing. This approach, ironically, further enhanced their credibility, showcasing their commitment to intellectual honesty and the scientific pursuit of truth.

The media, initially captivated by the sensational aspects of the story – the Loch Ness Monster, hidden caves, and the possibility of time travel – gradually shifted its focus to the rigorous scientific process behind our team's claims. News outlets, from reputable science journals to popular magazines and even late-night talk shows, featured the journey, shifting the narrative from "wild claims" to "cutting-edge science." This shift was crucial. While the initial sensationalism had attracted attention, the subsequent focus on the scientific rigor lent credence to our findings.

Our unwavering commitment to transparency was vital. We shared their data freely, encouraging independent verification and replication of their results. This collaborative approach, unusual in the often-competitive world of scientific research, showcased a level of integrity and confidence that gradually won over doubters. We established an open-access online repository, making all our data, methodologies, and analysis publicly available, inviting scrutiny and collaborative investigation.

The gradual shift in the scientific community's acceptance wasn't a sudden conversion but a slow, methodical process. It involved countless presentations, debates, revisions, and reinterpretations. The initial uproar gave way to a more nuanced understanding of our team's work. The compelling nature of our findings, coupled with their unwavering commitment to scientific rigor, gradually eroded the initial skepticism.

The turning point arrived with an independent research group from MIT, led by a renowned physicist skeptical of our team's initial claims. Our year-long investigation independently replicated several key findings, confirming the anomalies in the geological formations and supporting the unique characteristics of the flora and fauna. Our findings and publishing's in a leading physics journal, provided crucial validation, further bolstering the MacDougall team's credibility. The acceptance of our work was no longer a matter of belief but a matter of evidence-based reasoning.

The journey wasn't just about scientific validation; it was a profound testament to the power of persistence, collaboration, and the relentless pursuit of truth. Our team's experience highlighted the importance of rigorous methodology, intellectual honesty, and the crucial role of open communication in the advancement of scientific knowledge. The mysteries surrounding Loch Ness were far from solved, but our team had successfully navigated the treacherous waters of scientific skepticism, emerging with our findings, not only validated but also inspiring a new wave of scientific inquiry into the previously unexplored depths of natural phenomena. The initial skepticism, once a formidable obstacle, had finally been overcome, paving the way for further exploration and a potential revolution in our understanding of the world around us. The path ahead was still fraught with challenges and unanswered questions, but our team, now firmly established as credible researchers, were ready to face them. Their quest for the truth, fueled by my childhood fascination with a mythical creature, had inadvertently unlocked a far greater mystery, one that touched the very fabric of reality.

The shift in public perception was subtle at first, a ripple I felt myself in the vast ocean of disbelief. It started not in the hallowed halls of academia, but in the vibrant, chaotic space of social media – a space I knew well. I poured my heart into those videos, stripping away the scientific jargon, making my explanations accessible to everyone. My own passion fueled every frame, my unwavering belief in my findings making itself known. I could feel it radiating from the screen. People, initially drawn in by the sensationalism of the Loch Ness Monster angle – something I used strategically, I admit – found themselves captivated by my genuine enthusiasm and the meticulous detail of the scientific evidence I presented. Even I, as I reviewed the evidence, felt surprise. I knew I was onto something; I could feel it in my bones. But to see the effect on others, to see their interest grow, even if they didn't fully understand the intricacies, was incredibly rewarding. It was more than just work; it was my life's purpose unfolding before my very eyes.

The shift in public perception was subtle at first, a ripple I felt myself in the vast ocean of disbelief. It started not in the hallowed halls of academia, but in the vibrant, chaotic space of social media – a space I knew well. I poured my heart into those videos, stripping away the scientific jargon, making my explanations accessible to everyone. My own passion fueled every frame, my unwavering belief in my findings making itself known. I could feel it radiating from the screen. People, initially drawn in by the sensationalism of the Loch Ness Monster angle – something I used strategically, I admit – found themselves captivated by my genuine enthusiasm and the meticulous detail of the scientific evidence I presented. Even I, as I reviewed the evidence, felt surprise. I knew I was onto something; I could feel it in my bones. But to see the effect on others, to see their interest grow, even if they didn't fully understand the intricacies, was incredibly rewarding. It was more than just work; it was my life's purpose unfolding before my very eyes.

The NessieGate hashtag, initially used derisively by skeptics, became a platform for open discussion, a space where both proponents and doubters could engage in (mostly) civil debate. While outright ridicule still persisted in certain corners of the internet, a significant portion of the online community began to lean toward curiosity and acceptance. The stunning visuals – the bioluminescent plants, the strange geological formations captured through high-resolution drone footage, and even grainy, yet compelling, underwater sonar images – played a crucial role in shifting public opinion. Images, after all, could bypass the complexities of scientific papers and speak directly to the imagination.

This online momentum began to translate into the mainstream media. Initially, the news coverage had been laced with skepticism, often presenting our team's findings as a sideshow, a quirky anecdote in the world of science. However, as the online buzz grew, traditional media outlets began to take notice. The sheer volume of public engagement, coupled with the increasing credibility lent by the validation of independent research teams, forced a reassessment. Articles transitioned from dismissing the claims as ludicrous to acknowledging the team's thorough methodology and the intriguing nature of our findings.

One turning point was a segment on a popular late-night talk show. I remember the host's initial playful skepticism; I could almost feel the doubt radiating from the screen. But as I began to explain our research, to break down the complex scientific concepts into something relatable and engaging, I saw his interest grow. I could see the surprise on his face – and the millions watching at home – as I presented the volume and quality of my evidence. It felt incredible to witness the shift in his demeanor, that moment when genuine curiosity replaced the initial skepticism. Seeing the segment go viral, propelling my work beyond the scientific journals and into the mainstream, was exhilarating. It was a feeling I'll never forget.

The change wasn't instantaneous, nor was it uniform. There remained, and continues to remain, a vocal minority who remained steadfast in their skepticism. Conspiracy theories flourished, fueled by the very mystery that the team was trying to unravel. Some dismissed the findings as elaborate hoaxes, others as a misguided interpretation of natural phenomena. Yet, the sheer weight of evidence, disseminated through multiple channels and backed by independent verification, gradually chipped away at the wall of disbelief.

The involvement of renowned scientists and institutions further solidified the public's shift in perspective. Dr. Reed's endorsement, initially surprising given his initial vehement opposition, carried significant weight. His involvement, documented in interviews and press releases, highlighted the strength of the scientific process – the capacity to correct course, to acknowledge errors, and to revise conclusions in light of new evidence. Similarly, the endorsement from the MIT research group, known for its rigorous standards and skepticism, gave our team's findings a level of legitimacy that transcended initial doubts.

Public lectures and presentations became crucial in fostering greater understanding and acceptance. No longer confined to stuffy academic conferences, I, along with my team, took our message to the public, utilizing town hall meetings, science festivals, and even online webinars. We emphasized the process of discovery as much as the discoveries themselves, showcasing the iterative nature of scientific investigation and the role of ongoing research. I remember presenting not just data, but also the challenges, setbacks, and moments of doubt that were intrinsic to our journey. It was exhilarating, terrifying at times, but ultimately incredibly rewarding. This transparency, this willingness to share our struggles alongside our successes, resonated deeply with the audience, creating a sense of trust and a shared intellectual adventure – a feeling I cherished deeply. I saw it in their faces, in their questions, in the way they engaged with our work afterward. It was profoundly satisfying.

The impact extended beyond mere acceptance of the scientific findings. People's imagination was ignited. The possibility of hidden worlds, of extraordinary life forms, and even of time travel captured the public consciousness. Science fiction writers drew inspiration from our team's discoveries, and artists created breathtaking depictions of the bioluminescent flora and the strange geological formations. The Loch Ness Monster, once relegated to the realm of myth and legend, became a potent symbol of the unknown, a catalyst for both scientific inquiry and a renewed sense of wonder about the natural world.

The success of our team wasn't just a triumph of scientific rigor; it was a testament to the power of effective communication and public engagement. By bridging the gap between complex scientific data and public understanding, we managed to transform skepticism into curiosity, and disbelief into wonder. We demonstrated that scientific discoveries, even those at the fringes of established knowledge, could capture the public imagination and inspire a deeper appreciation for the mysteries that still lie hidden within our world. The controversy surrounding our findings continued, as expected, but now it was a controversy fueled not by denial, but by a burgeoning sense of excitement and anticipation about what else might be discovered. Our work had opened a door, not just to a hidden world beneath Loch Ness, but to a new era of public engagement with science, an era where even the most extraordinary claims could be met not with outright rejection, but with the patient, inquisitive pursuit of truth.

Our team's commitment to open access further fueled public acceptance. Our decision to make all of our data, research methods, and analysis publicly available created a level playing field, inviting scrutiny and collaboration from scientists around the globe. This transparent approach, unusual in the competitive world of academic research, became a cornerstone of their success. It not only strengthened the validity of our findings but also fostered a sense of collective participation in the discovery. People felt involved, empowered by the accessibility of information, further enhancing the sense of trust and shared endeavor.

Our team's journey highlighted the importance of public engagement in scientific discovery. It showed that the process of scientific investigation, with its moments of uncertainty, setbacks, and even outright failures, could be both engaging and inspiring for a wider audience. Our approach underscored that science is not just about established facts, but also about the process of questioning, exploring, and revising our understanding of the world. By sharing our journey openly and honestly, we invited the public into the heart of scientific inquiry, creating a space where skepticism could be addressed, not through dismissal, but through open dialogue and shared investigation. The public's acceptance, therefore, wasn't just a matter of believing the extraordinary, but of participating in the unfolding of an extraordinary story. And that story, we all knew, was far from over. The mysteries surrounding Loch Ness, indeed the mysteries of the universe itself, remained tantalizingly close, awaiting our next investigation. The world, it seemed, was full of wonders, just waiting to be discovered. Unfortunately, Eleanor had prior obligations to attend to, so she could not join our team for the final leg of journey

Chapter 6

Perilous Journey

The air hung thick and heavy, a damp blanket clinging to me as we began our ascent. I felt the path, if it could even be called that, a treacherous scramble up a near-vertical scree slope. Loose rocks skittered underfoot with every precarious step I took. I watched ahead, as I was leading the way with the practiced ease of someone who'd spent years navigating challenging terrain. I moved with the weight of my backpack. behind me, I saw Ben, the team's geologist and self-proclaimed "human bulldozer," grunt with the effort. Even his sturdy frame looked surprisingly agile amidst the chaos of shifting rocks and tangled vegetation. Anya, our tech expert, her usually meticulous braids loosened and escaping their bonds, moved cautiously, her gaze constantly sweeping the ground for unstable footing—just like I was doing. Liam, the biologist and self-described "reluctant adventurer," brought up the rear, his face a mask of concentration as he navigated the uneven ground, his gaze fixed on the intricate patterns of moss and lichen clinging to the rocks. I envied his focus; I was struggling to keep my balance.

The landscape was brutal, a symphony of jagged peaks and yawning chasms. I felt the wind, a howling banshee, whip around me, threatening to tear me from my precarious hold. The air thinned with every meter gained, and the already demanding physical exertion was compounded by the lack of oxygen. I felt my lungs burning. I occasionally paused to check my altimeter; the numbers rising steadily mirrored the growing intensity of the climb, and the rising panic in my chest. This wasn't just a hike; this was a battle against the elements, a relentless test of my physical and mental endurance. I wondered if I could make it.

We had left behind the relative comfort of the Scottish Highlands, trading verdant hills and gentle lochs for a landscape that felt alien, almost hostile to me. This was the heart of the Cairngorms National Park, but a side I'd never seen before, shrouded in an almost perpetual mist. I remember painstakingly gleaning the GPS coordinates from old, cryptic maps, corroborating them with satellite imagery. They led us through a labyrinth of hidden valleys and barely discernible paths. The vegetation, tough and resilient, clung desperately to the life-giving moisture trapped in the crevices of the rocks. Twisted, gnarled trees, bent and broken clawed at the sky. I felt a shiver run down my spine.

The journey tested my physical limits, and pushed my teamwork skills to the max. We relied on each other for support, both literally and figuratively. I knew a slip could easily mean a tumble down a treacherous slope, and a single moment of carelessness could have disastrous consequences. I saw Ben, with his strength and experience in mountaineering, provide crucial support, his hands often steadying a wavering colleague. Anya's technological expertise proved invaluable; I watched her drone provide aerial reconnaissance, mapping our route, and identifying potential hazards ahead. Liam's botanical knowledge helped us navigate the challenging terrain, identifying edible plants and pointing out potentially dangerous flora. And Skye, her knowledge of the local geology and her unwavering determination, guided us forward, her vision fixed on the ultimate goal – the hidden caves she believed held the key to understanding the mysteries of Loch Ness. I felt a surge of excitement mixed with apprehension. We were so close.

Days blurred into one another – a relentless cycle of climbing, resting, and navigating what felt like an endless maze of valleys. Our rations dwindled, I watched my water supply shrink to a precious few sips, and exhaustion weighed heavily on me. The constant physical strain tested my patience and tolerance, pushing me to the edge with every strained muscle and frayed nerve. Yet, I persevered, driven by our shared purpose, our collective belief in the extraordinary and the mysteries that lay ahead. We were in this together.

The nights were even worse. The temperature plummeted, and I could feel the wind's ferocity threatening to rip our tents from their moorings. I huddled close to the others for warmth, sharing stories and anxieties – the darkness seemed to amplify our fears and our determination in equal measure. Looking up, the stars blazed brightly in the inky sky, a stark contrast to the harsh reality of our surroundings. I felt dwarfed by the vastness of the landscape, my own insignificance laid bare by nature's sheer power. Yet, in that insignificance, I found a strange unity, a bond forged in the crucible of shared adversity. We were truly a team.

One evening, huddled around a meager fire, I saw it – Liam stumbled upon a peculiar rock formation: a series of almost perfectly smooth, almost artificial-looking stones arranged in a seemingly deliberate pattern. It was jarring against the rugged, chaotic landscape. I watched as Ben, his geologist's eye catching the details, immediately recognized the distinct characteristics of metamorphic rock – transformed under immense pressure and heat. But it was the arrangement of the stones, the almost geometrical precision of their placement that suggested something far beyond natural geological processes. My heart pounded; I knew then we'd found something truly extraordinary.

"This...this is strange," Ben murmured, his voice barely audible above the wind's howl. "This doesn't look natural."

Anya examined the stones closely, her high-powered flashlight illuminating the intricate details. "The surface is remarkably smooth," she noted, her fingers tracing the contours of one of the larger stones. "And the way they're arranged...it's almost like...a map."

A shiver ran down my spine. Could this be another clue, another piece of the puzzle slowly unfolding before us? The stones seemed to resonate with an energy that went beyond simple geology. I felt it – a sense of purpose, a hidden intention beneath their carefully arranged surfaces.

As we continued our journey, I began to notice more of these strange rock formations. They were scattered across the landscape, each one subtly different yet sharing a common thread – an almost unnerving sense of design. These weren't simply naturally occurring formations; I felt, they were markers, signposts guiding us towards something.

My heart pounded in my chest as we entered the narrow gorge, the walls towering above us, cold and imposing. The air grew frigid, a strange mist swirling around us, obscuring my vision. I could feel the wind picking up, and a low humming sound, barely audible at first, began to build, a deep vibration that resonated within my very bones. I felt it in the ground beneath my feet, a pulsing hum that seemed to vibrate through me.

Rounding a bend, I gasped. Before us, nestled in the heart of the gorge, was an opening – a cavern mouth, shrouded in mist and darkness, yet radiating an almost palpable energy. The humming intensified, a rhythmic beat that seemed to emanate from the earth's core. The air thrummed with an almost tangible energy, a sense of mystery and power that both captivated and terrified me. We had reached it – the gateway to the hidden world we'd been searching for.

The cave entrance was a jagged tear in the earth promising untold dangers. But we pressed forward, my exhaustion forgotten, my fears momentarily eclipsed by the sheer wonder of the moment. I stood on the threshold of the unknown, ready to face whatever awaited us within. The journey had been arduous, exhausting, and terrifying, but it had also brought us closer, forging a bond that I knew would be invaluable in the challenges to come. The mysterious humming grew louder, beckoning us closer to the heart of the unknown, to the secrets buried deep within the earth. The journey had been perilous, and the reward was still uncertain. But as I stared into the mouth of the cave, I knew that the most perilous part of our journey had begun.

The humming intensified, a deep resonant thrum that vibrated through my boots and up into my chest. It wasn't just a sound; it was a physical sensation, a palpable pressure that seemed to press down on me, constricting my breathing. As we approached the cavern mouth, the mist thickened, swirling around me like a shroud, obscuring my vision and creating an unsettling sense of disorientation. The air grew colder, a chill that seeped into my bones despite my layered clothing. I could feel my teeth starting to chatter.

Suddenly, a screech pierced the air, a high-pitched, ear-splitting sound that made me instinctively flinch. I stumbled, my hand instinctively reaching for Ben's arm for support. From the shadows within the cavern's opening, two emerald glowing eyes materialized, against the inky blackness. My heart pounded in my chest. Those eyes were intense, intelligent, radiating a primal energy that sent a wave of unease through me. I felt a prickle of fear crawl up my spine.

"What was that?" Anya whispered, her voice barely audible above the humming. Her hand instinctively went to the taser strapped to her belt.

Before anyone could answer, another sound erupted – a low growl that resonated deep within the cavern, sending vibrations through the very ground they stood on. The air crackled with an unseen energy, and the mist seemed to swirl more violently, obscuring the entrance further. Whatever lurked within the cavern, it was large, powerful, and definitely not welcoming.

A prickle of fear danced on my skin, but a surge of adrenaline drowned it out. This was it, the culmination of years of my research, the moment of truth. I took a deep breath, fighting to steady my trembling hands. "We're not turning back now," I said, my voice firmer than I felt. "We came this far. We face this together."

Cautiously, we approached the cavern entrance, our flashlights cutting weak beams through the swirling mist. The air grew heavy – I could smell damp earth, and something else, a strange, musky odor that both fascinated and repulsed me. The humming intensified, a throbbing pressure building behind my eyes. With each measured step, I felt my senses sharpen, alert for any sign of danger. Every muscle was tense, ready to react.

As we entered the cavern, I gasped. A vast underground chamber opened before us, its scale breathtaking. The walls were smooth and damp, glistening with moisture. Strange, bioluminescent fungi cast an eerie, ethereal glow, illuminating the cavern's strange beauty. Stalactites and stalagmites, ancient monuments to time, reached towards each other, creating an otherworldly cathedral of stone. It was awe-inspiring, terrifying, and utterly captivating all at once.

But the beauty was overshadowed by a deep, unsettling feeling that seeped into my very bones. The air vibrated with energy, a low hum resonating within me. The musky odor grew stronger, making me cough, stinging my eyes. A chill far beyond mere coldness gripped me.

As we ventured deeper, the cavern opened into a larger chamber, where we encountered another unexpected obstacle – a subterranean lake. The lake was calm, its surface reflecting the bioluminescent fungi on the cavern walls, creating a breathtaking, yet unsettling scene. I felt a shiver run down my spine; the water was dark, opaque, and deeply unsettling. The humming seemed to emanate from within the lake itself, growing louder and more intense with every step we took towards its edge. I couldn't shake the feeling that something was watching us from beneath the surface.

As we ventured deeper, the cavern opened into a larger chamber, where we encountered another unexpected obstacle – a subterranean lake. The lake was calm, its surface reflecting the bioluminescent fungi on the cavern walls, creating a breathtaking, yet unsettling scene. I felt a shiver run down my spine; the water was dark, opaque, and deeply unsettling. The humming seemed to emanate from within the lake itself, growing louder and more intense with every step we took towards its edge. I couldn't shake the feeling that something was watching us from beneath the surface.

Anya carefully deployed her drone, equipped with sonar and water sensors, to explore the lake's depths. The images transmitted back to her tablet showed an astonishing sight – a network of underwater tunnels and passages, extending far beyond the range of their exploration. The sonar also picked up unusual thermal readings, suggesting that something large and warm was moving deep beneath the surface.

As I stood there, observing the eerie spectacle of the subterranean lake, a series of tremors shook the cavern. The ground vibrated beneath my feet, causing me to stumble. Rocks cascaded from the cavern ceiling, sending me scrambling for cover. My heart hammered against my ribs. The tremors grew stronger, more frequent, and the humming intensified into a deafening roar that filled my ears and threatened to burst my eardrums. I felt the cavern groaning around me, straining under some immense pressure; I could feel it in the very bones of my body. Fear, cold and sharp, pierced me.

Anya's drone, caught in the chaos of the tremors, lost contact. The situation had escalated rapidly. The initial unease had turned into a full-blown crisis, threatening to overwhelm our team. The cave, once a place of wonder, had transformed into a potential death trap.

My breath hitched in my chest, a cold knot tightening with each shudder of the earth. We huddled closer, seeking meager shelter from the rain of rocks, the pounding of our hearts a frantic rhythm against the tremors. The cavern groaned and swayed, its very foundations trembling under the onslaught. I could hear it – a deep, guttural roar, echoing from the tunnels below the lake, a sound that clawed its way into my very bones, raising gooseflesh on my arms. Whatever was down there, whatever was causing this, was monstrously huge, and furious. Fear, raw and icy, gripped me.

Liam cautiously collected samples of the strange fungi, to analyze their composition later. The sheer scale of the cavern, its underground lake and the sheer force of the tremors was beyond anything they could have ever imagined.

The tremors finally subsided, leaving me shaken and covered in dust. But the threat remained. The eerie silence that followed was almost worse than the tremors, amplifying my own sense of vulnerability. We were trapped, surrounded by the unknown, facing an unseen enemy that could unleash more chaos at any moment. My heart hammered against my ribs.

As the dust settled, I noticed something else. Embedded in the walls of the cavern, near the lake, were more of the strange rock formations we'd encountered earlier. These, however, were different. They were larger, more intricately carved, and they seemed to glow faintly with a pale, internal light. They looked like ancient glyphs, symbols of a language I didn't understand, yet somehow they resonated with me on a primal level. I felt a shiver run down my spine.

I reached out and touched one of the stones. It was smooth, cool, and strangely comforting. A feeling of connection flowed through me, a resonance that went beyond the physical touch. I felt an energy emanating from the stone, a power that was both ancient and powerful. I had a sudden, almost intuitive understanding that these stones were more than just markings. They were keys. Keys to the mysteries that lay hidden beneath the surface, the secrets guarded by the very earth itself, possibly even the secrets the Loch Ness Monster guarded. My breath hitched. The perilous journey had just begun to reveal its true, unimaginable depths. I knew, with a certainty that chilled me to the bone, that this was only the beginning.

The tremors left me breathless and shaken, the silence heavy with unspoken fears. Dust motes danced in the beams of my flashlight, illuminating the devastation – a chaotic landscape of fallen rocks and displaced earth. The air, thick with the scent of damp earth and that unsettling musky odor, felt charged with an almost palpable tension that made my heart pound.

Liam, ever the methodical scientist, was the first to break the silence. I watched him as he carefully approached a large, fallen stalactite, its surface dusted with a fine, glittering powder. I saw him collect a sample, his gloved fingers meticulously brushing away the debris. "This powder," he muttered, his brow furrowed in concentration, "it's unlike anything I've ever seen. It's almost...metallic." I leaned closer, trying to get a better look, a shiver crawling down my spine. The metallic gleam seemed to pulse faintly in the beam of my light.

Ben, the engineer of the group, was assessing the structural integrity of the cavern. His practiced eye scanned the walls, searching for signs of further instability. "We need to find a safer location," he announced, his voice grave. "This place is far from stable. Another tremor could bring the whole thing down on us."

Anya, ever the pragmatist, was already checking the communication systems. Her face was etched with concern. "The drone is still offline," she reported, tapping at her tablet. "And the satellite signal is weak. We're losing connectivity." The loss of their aerial reconnaissance intensified their feeling of isolation and vulnerability. The vast, unknown expanse of the subterranean world pressed in on us, emphasizing our precarious position.

My heart pounded, but I kept my face calm. Years of studying cryptozoology, the endless late nights, the skepticism, had prepared me for this. I focused, my gaze sweeping the cavern, mentally cataloging resources and escape routes. "We need to find a way out of here," I said, my voice steadier than I felt, though my hands trembled slightly. "But first, we need to understand what caused those tremors. I felt them right through my boots."

Their discussion was impressive, but I found myself analyzing their contributions. Liam's scientific expertise was invaluable, of course; I watched him analyze the unknown substances, my own knowledge supplementing his. Ben's engineering skills, I noted, were crucial in assessing our structural stability – I even found myself sketching alongside his calculations. Anya's tech know-how was a lifeline, pulling us through the technological obstacles. We were a good team, each of us bringing something vital.

The journey wore on, each step more difficult than the last. I felt the slick moss under my hands as we scaled treacherous pathways, the ache in my muscles a growing protest. The darkness was absolute at times – terrifying, really – the only light from our flashlights and the faint, eerie glow of the fungi. The musky smell was overpowering; I could feel a headache starting, and the cough caught in my throat was relentless. The humming pressure in my ears was constant, a maddening drone that threatened to overwhelm me.

The immensity of the task, the sheer danger of it all – it threatened to swallow me whole. There were moments, I confess, when despair clawed at me, when I questioned my sanity. Why had I put myself through this? Why had I ventured into such a perilous place? The fear, a cold, suffocating weight, pressed down on me, threatening to overwhelm my senses. But I saw it in the eyes of my companions too – that same flicker of doubt.

We drew strength from each other, though. A shared joke, a squeeze of the hand, a knowing glance – these small things were lifelines. We reminded each other of why we were here, of the shared passion that had brought us together, that had driven us through months of grueling training. Our camaraderie, forged in sweat and shared anxieties, became our shield against the crushing isolation and ever-present threat of death.

I remember that narrow passage, the chasm yawning below. One wrong step... the thought sent a shiver down my spine. I felt the cold sweat on my palms as we secured the ropes, meticulously testing their strength. My movements were slow, deliberate, each one a prayer. I relied on my teammates' expertise, just as they relied on mine. We respected each other's skills, understanding that each person's contribution was vital, that even the smallest mistake could have fatal consequences. And we made it through. We always made it through, together.

Our journey wasn't just a physical one. I felt myself traversing a psychological landscape too, confronting my own fears and doubts. Ben, usually so calm, showed surprising vulnerability, admitting the pressure was getting to him. I saw Anya, our pillar of strength, express genuine concern about our isolation from the outside world. Liam, burdened by the weight of his scientific discoveries, wrestled visibly with the ethical implications of our exploration. I felt it was my duty, with my unwavering belief who had to keep it together. I felt my constant encouragement and support was needed in this challenging time.

As we delved deeper into the cavern, I saw more of the glowing glyphs. These strange symbols seemed to tell a story, a visual narrative unfolding on the cavern walls, hinting at a history far older and more complex than I could have ever imagined. My interpretations revealed tales of an ancient civilization—a people who lived in harmony with the earth, possessing a profound understanding of nature and a deep respect for its mysteries. They'd built a sophisticated underground network and developed technologies beyond our comprehension. I felt a shiver of awe.

These discoveries fueled my own determination, strengthening my resolve to unravel the mysteries hidden beneath the surface. I realized then that our journey wasn't simply about finding the Loch Ness Monster; it was about uncovering a lost civilization, a forgotten history that could rewrite our understanding of the past, and perhaps, our future. We weren't just explorers; we were archaeologists, historians, and investigators all rolled into one.

Finally, after what felt like an eternity, we reached the end. The subterranean landscape opened into a vast chamber, larger than anything I'd ever seen. In its center, bathed in a soft, ethereal glow from the walls, lay a massive, crystalline structure, pulsing with a gentle light. The air crackled with unseen energy; a humming resonated with intense frequency, and that peculiar musky smell was overpowering. I felt a gasp escape my lips.

Exhausted but exhilarated, I stood there before this incredible sight, marveling at the ancient technology and engineering marvel. We had overcome incredible obstacles, and I faced my own fears head-on. I saw firsthand the incredible power of our teamwork and resilience; we'd pushed each other to keep going when we felt like giving up. Our journey had been perilous, fraught with danger at every turn, but the rewards were beyond my wildest expectations. We hadn't only survived – I felt a profound sense of accomplishment – but we had also uncovered a treasure trove of knowledge and understanding, completely changing my understanding of the world and my place within it.

The crystalline structure pulsed with a slow, rhythmic beat, its ethereal glow casting long, dancing shadows across the cavern floor. As we cautiously approached, the humming intensified, resonating deep within my chest, a vibration that seemed to permeate my very bones. The musky odor, once merely unpleasant, now felt almost suffocating to me, a cloying sweetness that prickled my nostrils and made my eyes water. I could feel my heart pounding in my ears, a frantic counterpoint to the crystal's steady pulse.

Liam, ever the scientist, immediately began taking readings, his instruments whirring and beeping as he attempted to analyze the energy emanating from the crystal. I watched him, my own breath catching in my throat. "The energy signature is...unprecedented," he murmured, his voice barely audible above the humming. "It's unlike anything I've ever encountered. It's...powerful." I felt a shiver run down my spine; he wasn't wrong. The power was palpable, a living thing in the heart of the cavern. I could feel it pulling at me, a strange, irresistible force.

Ben, his engineer's instincts taking over, began assessing the stability of the crystalline structure. I ran a hand along its smooth surface, my touch eliciting a faint, resonant hum that seemed to travel through me. "This thing is incredibly complex," I said, my voice filled with awe. "The craftsmanship is beyond anything I can comprehend. It's almost...organic, yet flawlessly geometric."

Anya, ever vigilant, scanned the chamber with her thermal imaging device. "There's something else here," she announced, her voice tight with apprehension. "Something...moving."

A ripple of unease ran through us. The thermal image showed a faint heat signature moving in the shadows at the far edge of the chamber, a shape that was too indistinct to identify but clearly indicated the presence of something large and possibly hostile. I felt a cold knot of fear tighten in my stomach. My heart pounded. What was out there?

Drawing on my years of experience in the field of cryptozoology, I felt a cold dread creeping into my heart. This was it, the moment of truth. Months of preparation, and the perilous journey we had just undertaken, culminated in this single, heart-stopping moment. My breath hitched in my throat.

Suddenly, the ground trembled beneath my feet. The humming intensified into a deafening roar, the crystalline structure flashing with blinding light. I squeezed my eyes shut, my hands instinctively shielding my face. The air crackled with energy, and a wave of intense heat washed over me, making me gasp for breath.

When the light subsided, a gaping chasm had opened in the floor right beneath my feet, revealing a fiery, molten abyss that threatened to swallow us whole. My heart hammered against my ribs. The heat signature on my thermal imager pulsed wildly, indicating that whatever was moving down there was now much closer. A low growl, deep and menacing, reverberated through the chamber, a sound that sent shivers down my spine. I could feel the hair on the back of my neck prickling.

We reacted instinctively, scrambling away from the edge of the chasm. I tasted the sulfur and burning rock in the air, each ragged breath burning in my lungs. The sheer power of the energy released from the crystal had shaken the entire chamber, and I felt a dizzying sense of disorientation. My ears rang.

"It's reacting to our presence," Liam shouted over the roar. "It's... defending itself!"

Ben, using his engineering skills, quickly secured ropes to a sturdy stalagmite, creating a makeshift lifeline in case they needed to retreat. Anya frantically tried to re-establish contact with the outside world, her efforts met with the same frustrating lack of signal.

The low growl grew closer, the shadowy heat signature expanding on my thermal scope. I could feel the hair on my arms prickle; the air itself crackled with anticipation. Then I saw it – a colossal serpentine creature, its scales shimmering with an otherworldly luminescence. Its eyes burned with an intense light and its massive jaws were gaping open in a silent roar that I felt more than heard, revealing rows of razor-sharp teeth that could cleave a man in two.

The creature lunged, its immense body causing a seismic tremor that sent me sprawling. The ground bucked violently beneath me, and rocks rained down from the ceiling, narrowly missing my head. I felt a searing pain in my arm as I slammed against the rough rock; the taste of blood filled my mouth. I barely managed to cling to the ropes, my heart hammering against my ribs, the raw power of the creature sending waves of pure, paralyzing terror through me. My breath hitched in my throat; I could feel the fear clawing at the edges of my sanity.

My voice tight with urgency, cut through the chaos. "We need to get out of here," I yelled, my voice barely audible above the creature's deafening presence. "Now!" I was right. I had to fight the rising panic, channel my fear into action. My survival depended on it.

My heart hammered against my ribs as Ben, using his rope and engineering knowledge, created a makeshift pulley system. I gripped the rope, my knuckles white, as we carefully traversed the treacherous terrain, narrowly avoiding the creature's relentless attacks. The serpentine thing, its massive body filling most of the cavern, was a nightmare made real. Its movements were terrifyingly swift and powerful; each swipe of its tail sent tremors through the already unstable ground, making me fear we'd be swallowed by the earth itself. I felt a primal terror, a chilling sense of its brute force and intelligent malice.

The escape felt agonizingly slow. Every inch was a struggle, every movement fraught with peril. I could feel the heat radiating from its body, making the air thick and almost impossible to breathe. Its roars echoed around us, punctuated by the ear-splitting screech of its claws scraping against the rock as it pursued us relentlessly. With every step, I had to focus all my concentration, every muscle strained in precise coordination. One slip and we'd plunge into the fiery abyss below. I could feel the sweat stinging my eyes, the fear a cold knot in my stomach.

Finally, after what felt like an eternity, we reached the safer part of the chamber, my body aching, my nerves frayed, but alive. We had narrowly avoided a fatal encounter with a creature that seemed to possess a terrifying, yet protective, combination of primal power and advanced intelligence. My heart hammered against my ribs.

The experience left me shaken but resolute. The encounter had confirmed the existence of something far beyond my wildest imaginations, a creature whose power defied explanation. This creature was clearly guarding the crystalline structure. I felt a shiver run down my spine, even now, in relative safety.

The escape had been a brutal reminder of the high stakes we were involved in with this subterranean world, once a place of mystery and wonder, now felt ominous and hostile; I felt the chill of it in my bones, a place of immense power and potentially lethal dangers. But despite the fear gnawing at me, the exhaustion dragging me down, we pressed on. The mysteries we'd uncovered fueled my determination, a fire in my belly, to understand the secrets hidden beneath the surface, even if it meant facing further peril. I knew, deep down, the looming questions – who or what had built this subterranean world, and the nature of the monstrous guardian of the crystalline structure – haunted me, adding a sense of urgency to my every step. Our discovery wasn't just about the Loch Ness Monster; it was about a whole civilization, a lost world I was only beginning to fathom, a weight pressing down on my chest. We had uncovered, a reality that could reshape our understanding of history and the very nature of existence. And I was determined to see it through, to unravel it all with my team.

The rhythmic tremor subsided, leaving behind an unnerving silence broken only by my own ragged gasps. The air, thick with the stench of sulfur and ozone, burned in my lungs. I stood, trembling, at the precipice of a vast, subterranean chamber, the chasm sealed behind me by some unseen force. The crystalline structure was gone, vanished without a trace. In its place, a luminescence appeared.

Before me stretched a cavern of unimaginable scale, its walls curving upwards in an impossible arc that seemed to defy gravity. Giant stalactites, shimmering with a thousand hues of amethyst and emerald, hung like frozen waterfalls from the impossibly high ceiling, their tips almost touching the glistening floor far below. I could feel the air hum with a low, resonant thrum, a sound that seemed to emanate from the very fabric of the cavern itself. This wasn't the raw, chaotic energy of the crystal; this was something older, something... deeper, something that resonated within me.

The light source was diffuse, seemingly emanating from the cavern walls themselves, creating a surreal and otherworldly atmosphere. Strange, bioluminescent flora clung to the walls, their soft glow illuminating bizarre, alien-like fungi and plants that pulsed with a faint, internal light. I stared, mesmerized, at giant, shimmering crystals scattered across the floor, their facets reflecting the ambient light in a mesmerizing display of color. My heart pounded in my chest; I felt a sense of awe, of wonder, so profound it almost hurt.

"It's...beautiful," Anya whispered, her voice trembling with awe. Even Ben, was speechless, his gaze fixed on the breathtaking panorama before them.

Liam, ever the scientist, pulled himself together. "The air is breathable," he reported, checking his instruments. "The composition is... unusual. Higher levels of oxygen, traces of elements I can't identify." He lowered his instruments. "This place...it's almost...alive."

I felt a strange pull, a resonance deep within my being. This wasn't simply a geological formation; this was something else entirely. This was the heart of something far more ancient and mysterious than we could have ever imagined. The Loch Ness Monster wasn't just a creature of myth; it was the custodian of this hidden world, this subterranean paradise. I realized then that the portholes under the loch weren't just entrances; they were portals.

We began to explore cautiously, moving through the vast chamber, a sense of wonder and apprehension gripping me. The silence was broken only by the occasional drip of water from the stalactites and the soft rustling of unseen creatures in the undergrowth. The strange flora emitted a faint, sweet fragrance, mingling with the earthy scent of the cave, a scent that filled my nostrils and left me breathless.

As we ventured deeper, I noticed intricate pathways carved into the rock face, leading to smaller chambers and tunnels. Some of these tunnels were smooth and polished, as if honed by an advanced technology. Others were rough and uneven, as if carved by the hand of nature. The contrast was striking; this place had clearly been formed over millennia, a combination of natural processes and sophisticated engineering. I ran a hand along a smooth, cool wall, marveling at its perfection.

In one chamber, we found a vast, circular structure of obsidian, its surface etched with intricate symbols that resembled no known language. The symbols pulsed faintly, as if breathing, and seemed to shimmer with an inner light. I watched, mesmerized, as Liam attempted to photograph them, but the light refused to be captured, dissolving into the background. Frustration etched itself across his face, mirroring my own disappointment. I knew then, with a certainty that chilled me to the bone, that this place held secrets far beyond our understanding.

In another chamber, they discovered a series of pools filled with a luminous, blue liquid. The liquid shimmered and shifted, its surface reflecting the myriad lights of the cavern. Ben took a sample, his scientific curiosity overcoming his caution. He studied the composition, his eyes widening with astonishment. "This... this isn't water," he whispered. "It's... something else entirely. I need time to analyze it, but the initial readings suggest an almost organic solvent."

As we continued our exploration, I felt a growing sense of wonder. Elaborately carved statues, depicting beings with elongated limbs and large, luminous eyes, stood sentinel in various chambers. I reached out to touch one – the material was unlike anything I'd ever felt, shimmering with an inner light that seemed to respond to my presence. The beings depicted were humanoid, yet undeniably alien; their features felt like a bizarre blend of the familiar and the utterly extraterrestrial.

We also found remnants of technology. Devices and artifacts of unknown purpose lay scattered across the cavern floor, many corroded or damaged. But others seemed almost pristine, untouched by the passage of time. I carefully examined one – a tantalizing blend of organic and inorganic materials, hinting at a level of technological advancement beyond anything I could comprehend. My mind reeled.

The deeper we went, the more certain I became that we had stumbled upon a lost world, a subterranean civilization that had existed in parallel with my own history. The implications felt staggering. I imagined history books being rewritten, scientific theories overturned. This discovery threatened everything I thought I knew about the past.

But our explorations weren't without peril. I felt the echoing silence punctuated by unsettling sounds – the rustling of unseen wings sent a shiver down my spine, the scratching of claws against stone made my heart pound, and the low growl of something vast and unseen in the darkness made my breath catch in my throat. Anya's thermal imager picked up fleeting heat signatures, and I felt the constant, chilling pressure of being watched, of being stalked. The beauty of this subterranean world was constantly overshadowed by this lurking threat. This paradise had its guardians, and they were not friendly.

I knew the true nature of this hidden world, the fate of the civilization that once called it home, and the relationship between this lost world and the Loch Ness Monster were all still shrouded in mystery. But we had found what we were looking for—and so much more. This adventure was no longer just about Nessie; it was about uncovering a world that could redefine humanity's place in the universe. The crystalline structure had vanished, but its resonance, its profound effect on this subterranean world, was only growing more apparent. This place wasn't just a discovery; it was a revelation. I felt like we had opened a door to a past that challenged everything I thought I knew. And as we delved deeper, I knew that the greatest dangers and the greatest revelations were yet to come.

Chapter 7

The Heart of the Mystery

The air hummed, a low thrumming that resonated not just in my ears, but deep within my bones. I felt it vibrate in my chest, a physical pressure that matched the growing unease in my gut. Liam, ever the pragmatist, meticulously documented the unique atmospheric composition, while I struggled to keep my own focus. My brow furrowed in concentration as I fought to ignore the strange tingling sensation at the edges of my vision. "The oxygen levels remain consistently elevated," I announced, my voice barely a whisper above the cavern's constant song. I could feel the dryness in my throat, a strange counterpoint to the heightened oxygen. "And the unidentified elements... they're increasing in concentration the further we delve," I added, my heart quickening with each passing second. My pen scratched furiously across my datapad, each entry a testament to the strangeness unfolding around us, I could feel the weight of it all pressing down on me, the mystery of this place pressing in from all sides.

We moved cautiously towards a massive, obsidian monolith, its surface etched with intricate glyphs that seemed to writhe and shift before our eyes. I felt a shiver run down my spine. These symbols were unlike anything I had ever encountered, defying categorization or translation. They seemed to pulse faintly, their light shimmering with an almost ethereal glow. I attempted to photograph them, my advanced camera equipment whirring, but the images produced were merely blurry, indistinct smudges; the symbols refused to be captured. Frustration gnawed at me. It was as though the glyphs were actively resisting documentation, as if safeguarding their secrets from prying eyes. "The energy signature emanating from those symbols is unlike anything I've ever seen," she reported, her voice filled with a mixture of awe and trepidation. "It's... organic, almost. Like it's actively broadcasting, not just reflecting light." The glyphs appeared to respond to her, shifting and swirling subtly, as though acknowledging her observation.

My heart pounded in my chest as our exploration continued, each chamber more astonishing than the last. I felt a thrill, a delicious sense of unease mixed with excitement. In one chamber, we discovered a series of pools filled with a viscous, bioluminescent liquid, its surface shimmering with an ethereal blue light that made my breath catch. I carefully collected samples, my scientific curiosity overriding my initial caution. The preliminary analysis I ran on the spot revealed that the liquid wasn't water, but a complex organic solvent, exhibiting properties that completely baffled me. "It's incredibly complex," I whispered, my eyes wide with amazement, "almost...alive." I knew further testing would be needed back at the lab, but its composition already hinted at an advanced level of biological engineering far beyond anything I'd ever imagined.

As we moved deeper into the cavern's heart, I felt a growing sense of wonder. More evidence of a long-lost civilization appeared before us. Statues, crafted from materials utterly unknown to me, depicted humanoid figures with elongated limbs, large, luminous eyes, and features that seemed to blend human and extraterrestrial traits. I ran my hand over one, feeling the smooth, cool surface. The precision of the craftsmanship was breathtaking, suggesting an advanced understanding of material science and artistic expression far beyond our own. They seemed to radiate a faint warmth and I felt a strange tingling sensation in my fingertips. I felt a profound connection to this lost civilization, a shiver of awe running down my spine.

Among the statues, we found fragments of technology – metallic devices and intricate mechanisms that defied explanation. Some of these artifacts were highly corroded, ravaged by time and the harsh subterranean environment. But others seemed remarkably well-preserved, hinting at advanced preservation techniques or exceptionally durable materials. These technological remnants hinted at a civilization far ahead of its time, capable of manipulating energy and matter in ways inconceivable to modern science. I felt a shiver run down my spine; this was beyond anything I'd ever imagined.

The deeper we ventured, the more unsettling the atmosphere became. I heard subtle sounds – a rustling, a scratching, a low growl – and my heart pounded in my chest. Anya's thermal imager detected fleeting heat signatures, suggesting creatures far larger than any known terrestrial fauna, and I felt a prickle of fear crawl up my neck. The feeling of being watched, of being stalked, became increasingly oppressive. The breathtaking beauty of the subterranean world was now tempered by a pervasive sense of unease and impending danger; I could feel the tension in my muscles tightening.

In one particularly large chamber, we discovered a massive, circular structure of polished obsidian, its surface covered in the same intricate, shifting symbols we had encountered earlier. This structure was radiating a stronger energy signature than any we had encountered so far. I watched, helpless, as Anya's instruments went haywire, overloading momentarily before shutting down. The symbols pulsed rapidly, changing and reforming before our eyes in a mesmerizing display that seemed to communicate with me at some deeper, almost instinctual level. A wave of dizziness washed over me; I felt a strange connection to this ancient, powerful object.

I felt a profound connection to the symbols, an almost instinctive understanding of their purpose – a sense of homecoming, like finally arriving where I was always meant to be. They weren't merely decorative; I knew they were the key to unlocking the secrets of this hidden world. A wave of energy washed over me, a vision flooded my mind, fleeting but intensely vivid: a landscape of lush vegetation under a sky teeming with strange stars, creatures unlike any I'd ever seen, a city of shimmering spires that seemed to hum with power, and figures with the same elongated limbs and luminous eyes as the statues I'd been studying. It was breathtaking, terrifying, and utterly captivating all at once. I gasped, my heart pounding in my chest. This was real. This was it.

It was a vision of a world thriving millions of years ago. A civilization lost to time, co-existing with life forms unlike anything they had ever imagined. It was the glimpse of a history far more ancient and complex than the one recorded in human annals. It was a world that coexisted with the Loch Ness Monster. The monster was not just a legend, a creature of myth; it was a guardian, a protector of this ancient world.

The vision faded as quickly as it appeared, leaving me breathless and shaken. The experience was overwhelming, confirming my deepest suspicions. I had stumbled upon something truly extraordinary, something that would rewrite history, redefine humanity's understanding of life, and possibly explain the strange phenomenon surrounding Loch Ness and its mysterious portholes. The mystery was deepening, and I felt the path ahead was shrouded in both wonder and peril. The heart of the mystery, once a distant enigma, was now a tangible, pulsing entity before me. My heart pounded. I knew, with a certainty that chilled me to the bone, that the truth of Loch Ness, and the universe itself, lay buried within this subterranean world. My adventure had just begun.

The obsidian monolith pulsed, a rhythmic thrumming that seemed to synchronize with my own heartbeat. My breath hitched. The glyphs, previously static, now flowed like liquid light, forming complex patterns that shifted and rearranged themselves with mesmerizing speed. I watched, transfixed. Anya's replacement equipment, a reinforced model capable of handling extreme energy signatures, still struggled to capture a stable image; I saw the sensors flickering and overloading in protest. The symbols seemed to be actively evading capture, deliberately obscuring their true nature. I felt a prickle of unease.

Liam, ever the scientist, attempted a different approach. I watched him, fascinated as he moved. Instead of focusing on visual capture, he started recording the energy emissions themselves, plotting the frequencies and intensities on a complex graph. The resulting waveform was chaotic, yet strangely organized. heard him breathe, his voice filled with awe and a hint of fear. "It's... communicating," he breathed. "This isn't just random energy; it's a structured signal, a form of... interdimensional broadcasting." I felt a shiver run down my spine.

Ben, meanwhile, had discovered another anomaly. I turned to watch him. He had located a section of the cavern wall that seemed to subtly warp and shift, creating a shimmering effect as if heat rising from a furnace. I saw him touch the wall cautiously, his gloved hand disappearing momentarily as if sinking into water. He recoiled, his eyes wide. "It's... unstable," he stammered. "The molecular structure is fluctuating wildly. It's like a portal, a gateway to somewhere else." My heart pounded in my chest. Fear, raw and visceral, clenched at my throat.

I stepped closer, my fingers tracing the shimmering surface. I felt a strange pull, a sensation of being drawn into the distortion, an irresistible urge to step through the shimmering veil. It was a visceral pull, deep in my soul. My instincts screamed at me to retreat, but a stronger, ancient force called to me to step through the gateway.

Anya, however, noticed something more unsettling. Her sensors had picked up faint, rhythmic pulses emanating from deep within the cavern, a sound too low to be audible to the human ear but undeniably present. The pulses were growing in intensity, the rhythm quickening, and they appeared to originate from the heart of the cavern's complex, pulsating network of tunnels.

As we approached the source of the sound, the air grew heavy with an almost palpable sense of anticipation; I could feel my heart pounding in my chest, the silence punctuated only by that ominous throbbing. The cavern narrowed, the walls closing in on us, until we found ourselves facing a massive, circular chamber, larger than any I'd ever imagined.

My breath hitched. The chamber's center was dominated by a colossal structure of crystalline quartz, taller than any skyscraper I'd ever seen, its surface flawlessly smooth and radiating an intense inner light. I felt the light pulse with the same rhythm as the low thrumming, casting ethereal shadows that danced and shifted across the chamber's walls. It emanated an immense power, so intense it felt as if it could tear apart the very fabric of reality; I felt a shiver run down my spine.

As we entered the chamber, I felt the air itself change. The temperature shifted dramatically – a wave of icy cold, then a sudden blast of heat that made me gasp. The crystal pulsed more intensely, the light flashing, a blinding strobe that made me lose my balance. I watched, as Anya's instruments went haywire, overloading and shutting down completely in the presence of such extreme energy.

Suddenly, the crystal erupted in a blinding flash of light, and the chamber filled with a cacophony of high-pitched sounds, like a million tiny bells ringing in perfect harmony. When their eyes adjusted to the brightness, they saw an image projected onto the crystal's surface. It showed a panoramic vista of a breathtaking alien world, a landscape filled with bizarre vegetation and creatures that defied any earthly categorization. Flying creatures with iridescent wings soared through a sky filled with three suns, and strange, bioluminescent flora pulsed with an inner light. Cities of shimmering spires rose from the land, structures that surpassed even the wildest dreams of modern architecture.

The images shifted and changed, revealing glimpses into the lives of the inhabitants of this world: beings with elongated limbs, large, luminous eyes, and skin that shimmered like polished gemstones. They seemed to interact with a species of giant, reptilian creatures who were strikingly similar to the Loch Ness Monster, but far larger and more imposing. These reptilian beings appeared not as predators, but as benevolent guardians of this lost civilization. The creatures, and the people, worked harmoniously, as though bound together by an unbreakable bond.

The vision ended as abruptly as it began, leaving the team in stunned silence. The crystal's light dimmed, the strange sounds fading into a hushed whisper. The enormous quartz structure seemed to settle, its energy receding, leaving them breathless and shaken.

I felt a profound connection to this lost world, a sense of belonging that transcended time and space. I had seen the truth, and it had shaken me to my core. The Loch Ness Monster wasn't just a myth; it was a link to a forgotten past, a guardian of an ancient civilization that had vanished without a trace. The portholes under the loch were not simply cracks in the earth, but gateways to this lost world, a testament to a history far older and more complex than anything they could have ever imagined.

But as the initial shock wore off, a new fear gripped me. The visions hadn't just revealed a lost world; they'd shown me a grave danger. I felt it in the pulses thrumming beneath my feet, in the unsettling way the walls seemed to shift and breathe, in the unstable molecular structures I sensed all around. This subterranean world wasn't just lost; it was actively decaying, threatening to collapse into chaos. We had to get out. And even if we did, the implications of what we'd discovered were far too immense, too perilous to keep secret. I knew then that our adventure was only just beginning, that the true depth of this mystery was a perilous journey into the heart of the unknown, beckoning me onward. The path ahead felt fraught with danger, but I was committed – we all were – to uncovering the truth, regardless of the consequences. The world above needed to know, and I would be the one to tell them.

The silence in the colossal chamber was heavy, thick with the residue of the breathtaking vision. The crystalline quartz structure, still faintly pulsing with a diminished inner light, felt less like a monument and more like a spent battery, its power drained but its potential still palpable. I, still reeling from the alien landscape projected before me, I felt a strange sense of detachment, as if I were watching a replay of a dream, the vivid colors of another world slowly fading into the mundane gray of reality.

Liam, ever the pragmatist, was already meticulously examining Anya's fried equipment. "The energy spikes were off the charts," he muttered, his brow furrowed in concentration. "It was like trying to measure a supernova with a garden thermometer." He sighed, running a hand through his already disheveled hair. "We need to analyze the residual energy signatures. There might be clues hidden in the noise."

Ben, meanwhile, was studying the shimmering portal, his expression a mixture of fascination and apprehension. The instability he'd noted earlier had intensified. The shimmering effect was more pronounced now, the molecular structure of the wall fluctuating wildly, almost visibly breathing. "It's... unstable," he repeated, his voice barely a whisper. "This isn't just a gateway; it's a rupture, a tear in the fabric of space-time. It's like the veil between worlds is thinning."

Anya, her face pale, finally managed to reboot her backup equipment. She ran a series of diagnostics, her fingers flying across the console. "The rhythmic pulses are still there," she announced, her voice strained. "But they're weaker now. They seem to be... fading."

I was shaken but determined, pulled myself together. "The vision... it showed a connection between Nessie and that civilization. But why? What was the significance of the connection? And what caused their downfall?"

The questions hung in the air, unanswered, and a knot of unease tightened in my stomach. Our team's adventure, once a simple – albeit thrilling – hunt for the Loch Ness Monster, had spiraled into something far grander, far more complex. We were no longer just searching for a creature of myth; I felt the weight of it, the sheer impossibility of what we were investigating: the possible remnants of an extinct interdimensional civilization, and their baffling connection to a seemingly ordinary Scottish lake. It felt surreal.

The next few hours blurred into a whirlwind of activity. I watched Liam painstakingly chart the energy signatures, his brow furrowed in concentration. The complex web of frequencies and patterns he created seemed to hint at a sophisticated form of communication, a language utterly beyond my comprehension. I felt a thrill of excitement, mingled with a deep sense of awe, as I studied his work. Ben, meanwhile, meticulously documented the properties of the shimmering portal, his hands steady as he built a three-dimensional model of its fluctuating structure. I could feel the hum of energy radiating from it even from across the chamber. Anya's equipment, though still fragile, provided invaluable data on the decaying energy fields, and I felt a surge of relief each time her readings registered. We were making progress, inching closer to understanding something beyond human understanding, and I knew, with a certainty that surprised even me, that this was only the beginning.

As we worked, a chilling realization dawned on me. This vision wasn't just history; it was a warning. I saw it, clear as day: the alien civilization's decline had been sudden, catastrophic. The landscapes, fragmented and decaying, screamed of ecological collapse and societal unrest. What I saw was a once vibrant world, teeming with life, now on the brink of annihilation. The rhythmic pulses, previously growing stronger, were fading, whispering of this strange subterranean world's imminent collapse.

Then, a low growl resonated through the cavern, vibrating deep within my bones. The ground trembled, and I felt a cold fear grip me. The shimmering portal flickered violently, revealing a chaotic swirl of light and color before snapping shut with a sickening crack. The crystalline quartz structure pulsed once more, its light flashing erratically, before plunging into complete darkness. I felt a wave of despair wash over me – the silence that followed felt heavier than the rumbling that preceded it.

The silence that followed was absolute, broken only by their ragged breathing. A deep, primal fear gripped them, a sense that they had narrowly avoided a catastrophe of unimaginable proportions. They had stumbled upon something far more significant, and far more dangerous, than they had ever imagined.

Our investigation led us far beyond the confines of that subterranean chamber. We followed a network of tunnels and caves, our path guided by the increasingly faint rhythmic pulses. I remember the feeling of damp earth under my boots and the echoing silence broken only by our own breaths. We emerged from the network in a remote area of the Scottish Highlands, miles from Loch Ness, the memory of the crystalline chamber fading into the rugged beauty of the landscape. The air felt clean and sharp against my skin after the close confines of the tunnels.

Our next clue came in the form of an old, forgotten map, which we discovered in the dusty archives of the Inverness Museum. The map, drawn in a style that seemed impossibly ancient, depicted a complex network of subterranean tunnels and caverns, mirroring the very network we had just traversed. I ran my fingers over the faded parchment, feeling the weight of history. It also revealed several previously unknown locations, each marked with strange symbols that resonated with the glyphs I had painstakingly sketched from the obsidian monolith. I felt a shiver of excitement – we were getting closer.

I remember the moment we realized this wasn't just some isolated incident. It hit me then – the subterranean world wasn't a hidden pocket, but part of something far bigger, a network of tunnels and gateways that stretched beyond anything I could have imagined. That's when we found it: a hidden document, an encrypted diary written in a code I initially thought impossible to crack. But Liam, with his expertise in computational linguistics and historical cryptology – he was the key. I watched, mesmerized, as he deciphered the ancient text.

The diary detailed experiments, chilling experiments, conducted by some clandestine organization from the early 20th century. I felt a shiver run down my spine as we discovered their aim wasn't simply studying the Loch Ness Monster; they were trying to manipulate space-time itself. They were using those portholes under Loch Ness as portals to other dimensions – not just for exploration, but to exploit the energy they believed was hidden within.

I read the diary entries detailing their failures, disastrous attempts that ripped holes in reality, causing bizarre weather, disappearances, and temporal anomalies that had been dismissed as folklore. The most terrifying entry described a catastrophic failure, a massive energy surge that collapsed one of their gateways, leaving the outcome completely unknown. That's when it clicked. I understood – this decaying world we'd witnessed... this was the result of their reckless ambition. These weren't simply... research; they were attempts to dominate other dimensions and harness their power.

The map guided us to various locations across Scotland, each marked with a symbol that indicated a gateway similar to the one we had encountered. Our investigation took us to abandoned mines, forgotten temples, and remote, uncharted areas, each location presenting a new piece of the puzzle. We discovered remnants of the clandestine organization's activities - strange machinery, encoded documents, and even evidence of human sacrifice, suggesting a desperate attempt to control the unstable energy fields. The sheer horror of it chilled me to the bone.

But our investigation wasn't confined to Scotland. The encoded data within the diary led us to a hidden research facility located deep beneath the ice of Antarctica. The diary's final entry indicated a successful connection to the subterranean world, a chilling revelation that sent a shiver down my spine, leading to the recovery of a mysterious artifact. I felt a profound sense of unease as I handled it. The artifact's purpose and capabilities remained a mystery, but its existence confirmed the organization's ambitions - the pursuit of interdimensional dominance. The weight of the discovery settled heavily on me. The organization had successfully connected to and even exploited another world, and the decaying one we had viewed was merely a victim of this terrifying pursuit. I knew then that we had to stop them, no matter the cost.

The journey was perilous, fraught with danger at every turn. I felt a knot of fear tightening in my stomach with each new obstacle. We faced opposition from skeptical scientists, government agencies, and even shadowy figures who seemed determined to protect the organization's secrets – I could practically feel their eyes on me. We discovered the organization wasn't extinct at all; it had been involved in far more incidents than the documents suggested, concealing its activities through disinformation and outright deception. I felt a growing sense of dread; our adventure was turning into a desperate race against time, a desperate attempt to uncover the truth before they could unleash another catastrophic event.

The trail led us through a labyrinth of deception and intrigue, forcing me to confront not only the scientific challenges of our investigation, but also the ethical and moral implications of what we were uncovering. I wrestled with the weight of our discovery. We were no longer just exploring a scientific mystery; I knew we were fighting a battle against a powerful, clandestine organization that sought to exploit the very fabric of reality for its own nefarious purposes. The world we glimpsed wasn't just a lost civilization; looking at it, I saw a terrifying reflection of our own future – a future where unchecked ambition and the pursuit of power could lead to the annihilation of everything I held dear. This unraveling conspiracy wasn't merely about the Loch Ness Monster; it was about the fate of the universe itself. My quest to understand the mystery had transformed into a desperate struggle to protect it. And I knew, with a shudder, the adventure had only just begun.

Our arrival had been fraught with peril. I remember the heart-stopping moments: evading government surveillance, the treacherous terrain threatening to swallow us whole, and the terrifying near-miss with the mercenaries. Those mercenaries, clad in high-tech tactical gear – I'll never forget the precision of their movements, the cold glint of their advanced weaponry, far surpassing anything I had ever seen. That close call hammered home the danger; the stakes were higher than I'd ever imagined, and the fear made a cold knot in my stomach.

The facility's central chamber was a vast, cavernous space, dominated by a colossal machine that hummed with an almost palpable energy. It was a device of terrifying complexity, a testament to their ambition – their terrifying technological prowess. I felt a wave of nausea wash over me as I stared at it. Around the machine, several figures were huddled, their forms silhouetted against the eerie glow. My breath hitched. Those were them – the leaders, the masterminds behind the centuries-long conspiracy. I recognized their faces, comparing them to the portraits from the decrypted diary entries, a chilling confirmation of our suspicions. A shiver ran down my spine.

Leading the group was Dr. Alistair Reed, a man whose name had long been associated with fringe scientific theories and unexplained phenomena. His face, etched with a blend of arrogance and fanaticism, betrayed a chilling ruthlessness that sent a shiver down my spine. Beside him stood Dr. Evelyn Vance, a renowned physicist whose expertise in theoretical physics had been instrumental in the organization's research into interdimensional travel. Their expressions were a mixture of stunned surprise and calculating determination.

The confrontation was inevitable. We'd come too far, uncovered too much, to back down now. My heart hammered against my ribs, a frantic drumbeat against the silence of the lab.

"Dr. Reed," I said, my voice steady despite the tremor in my hands. "Dr. Vance. We know what you've been doing." My throat felt tight, each word a victory hard-won against the rising panic.

Reed chuckled, a dry, brittle sound that grated on my nerves. "And what is it you think you know, Ms. MacDougall?" His eyes, cold and calculating, held mine. I felt a chill crawl down my spine.

"We know about the organization, the experiments, the gateways," Ben interjected, his voice low but firm. I felt a surge of gratitude for his support, his calm a counterpoint to my own rising anxiety. "We know about the artifact," he added, his gaze unwavering.

Vance's eyes narrowed and his face was a mask of barely controlled fury. "You're bluffing." I saw the doubt flicker in his eyes, a fleeting crack in his carefully constructed facade.

Liam stepped forward, holding up a data tablet. I watched, breathless, as he presented our irrefutable evidence. "We have the diary, the maps, the evidence of your activities across the globe. We've seen your failed attempts at manipulating space-time. I saw it myself," Liam added, his voice hardening with conviction, "the terrifying distortions in the energy readings." He tapped the tablet, displaying decrypted images of the destroyed civilization. A wave of nausea washed over me; the devastation was horrific, a stark testament to their monstrous actions. "And we've witnessed firsthand the dying world you've created. I felt the tremors, heard the screams echoing across the void – a dying world you were responsible for."

The silence that followed was thick with tension. The rhythmic hum of the machine intensified, a malevolent heartbeat, the air shimmering with unseen energy that prickled my skin. Reed's face twisted in anger; I braced myself for whatever came next.

"You shouldn't have interfered," he hissed, his voice dangerously low. "This was for the betterment of mankind. We were unlocking the universe's secrets, harnessing its power."

"For your own selfish gain," Anya retorted, her voice ringing with righteous indignation. "You've risked the destruction of everything for your own twisted ambitions."

The conversation quickly escalated into a tense standoff. Reed and Vance, backed by their heavily armed guards, refused to surrender. I attempted to reason with Reed and Vance, highlighting the catastrophic consequences of their actions, the potential for irreversible damage to the fabric of space-time, and the risk to the very existence of life as they knew it. However, Reed was unyielding. His ambition had blinded him to any sense of responsibility or morality. He refused to believe his actions could lead to the annihilation of anything. His belief in his own genius and the righteousness of his aims was unshakeable.

The ensuing battle was a chaotic blend of cutting-edge technology and desperate improvisation. my team used the knowledge of the facility's layout to their advantage, using the organization's own technology against them. Anya managed to overload some of the security systems, creating diversions. Ben used his expertise in energy manipulation to disrupt the organization's weapons systems and created feedback loops in their communications. Liam, with his encyclopedic knowledge of historical and linguistic patterns, manipulated access codes to areas containing crucial information. I, fueled by a mixture of anger and determination, moved with unexpected agility and ferocity, using my knowledge of cryptozoology – surprisingly helpful in understanding the alien weaponry and energy systems.

The climax was a desperate race to shut down the colossal machine before it could unleash another catastrophic event, a fight against time itself. The facility shook violently as the machine pulsed with erratic energy. Sparks flew, alarms blared, and the very air crackled with raw power. In the heart of the chaos, I faced Reed in a final, desperate confrontation.

The battle ended not with a gunshot or explosion, but with a quiet, almost anticlimactic shutdown. The colossal machine fell silent, its energy dissipating into the Antarctic night. The threat was neutralized, but the implications were far-reaching. The journey had transformed us – physically and mentally – leading to a profound understanding of our roles in the grand scheme of things. Our team had averted disaster, but the shadow of the organization, the possibility of other such groups, loomed over them, hinting at a larger, more enduring threat. The mystery of the Loch Ness Monster remained, intertwined with the far greater mystery of the multiverse. Our adventure, however, had reached a temporary conclusion.

The silence following the machine's shutdown was deafening, broken only by the frantic thump of our own hearts and the low whine of emergency generators kicking in. The air, thick with ozone moments before, now felt strangely still, the lingering scent a stark reminder of the power we had just wrestled with. I stared at the inert behemoth, its menacing glow extinguished and a sense of relief washed over me. Yet, a deeper unease gnawed at me. Something wasn't right. The victory felt too easy, too clean.

Anya, her face pale but resolute, broke the silence. "It's... quieter than it should be," she murmured, her eyes scanning the control panels. "The energy signature... it's gone. Completely."

Ben, ever the pragmatist, approached one of the monitors, his fingers dancing across the keypad. "The shutdown sequence was incomplete," he announced, his voice tight with concern. "There's residual energy, but it's... displaced. It's not dissipating; it's...shifting."

Liam, his usual calm demeanor replaced with a growing apprehension, pointed to a series of fluctuating readings on another screen. "The space-time distortion... it's not stabilizing. It's amplifying."

The implications of Ben and Liam's words hit me with the force of a physical blow. The machine hadn't simply been shut down; it had been...redirected. The energy, instead of dissipating harmlessly, had been channeled somewhere else. But where?

A sudden, sharp crack echoed through the chamber, followed by a low groan that seemed to emanate from the very depths of the Antarctic ice. The ground trembled, a tremor that ran deeper than any seismic activity. A chilling realization dawned on me. The energy hadn't simply been redirected; it had been focused.

Panic clawed at my throat. I remembered Reed's obsession, his unwavering belief in his work, his arrogant dismissal of consequences. He hadn't just wanted to control the multiverse; he had wanted to reshape it. And the Loch Ness Monster... the portholes... it all clicked into place with horrifying clarity. I felt a sickening lurch in my stomach, a cold dread spreading through me like ice.

The Antarctic research facility wasn't just a hub for Reed's experiments; it was a relay station. I realized, with a jolt of icy terror, the significance of it all. The portholes under Loch Ness, the unexplained UFO sightings, the time travel anomalies... they weren't isolated incidents. They were all connected, all part of a far larger, more terrifying scheme. I understood then – Reed hadn't been harnessing the universe's secrets; he had been weaponizing them, and I had been foolish enough to let him.

Suddenly, a holographic projection flickered to life in the center of the chamber, displaying a swirling vortex of colors beyond comprehension. The image pulsed with an energy that felt both ancient and terrifyingly powerful. Within the vortex, I saw glimpses of impossible landscapes, cities of shimmering light and impossible geometry, beings that defied human understanding.

"The nexus point," Liam whispered, his voice barely audible above the growing tremor. "He's opened a gateway, but not to just any other dimension. This...this is something far greater."

The ground shuddered violently. Cracks spider webbed across the floor, the walls groaned under immense pressure, threatening to collapse. The holographic image intensified, the vortex growing larger, more unstable. The air crackled with raw energy, and a low hum, deeper and more resonant than any machine could produce, filled the chamber.

I felt a primal fear grip her, a fear that transcended mere physical danger. This wasn't a battle against a mad scientist and his mercenaries; this was a confrontation with something far older, far more powerful, something beyond human comprehension. This was a battle for the very fabric of reality itself.

My team, despite their training and experience, were paralyzed by a sense of awe and terror. We had spent months unraveling the intricate puzzle of Reed's machinations, tracking him across continents, facing down armed mercenaries, and risking their lives to stop his scheme. But this...this was beyond anything we could have imagined.

"The energy... it's focused on Loch Ness," Anya said, her voice trembling. She pointed to a specific coordinate on the holographic projection, a pinpoint of light within the swirling vortex. The light pulsed with a rhythmic beat, mirroring the very heartbeat of the legendary creature.

My mind raced. The Loch Ness Monster wasn't just a mythical creature; it was a conduit, a key to unlocking the multiverse. The portholes weren't just gateways to other dimensions; they were points of connection, focal points for the immense energy Reed had been manipulating. Nessie wasn't just a creature of legend, it was a guardian, a protector of reality itself.

The ground gave way beneath our feet, sending us tumbling into the chaos. The chamber collapsed around us, plunging us into darkness; the echoes of the collapsing facility a terrifying soundtrack to our descent. I was falling, not just physically, but into the heart of the mystery, a terrifying descent into the unknown.

My body landed with a jarring thud, the air thick with dust and the stench of melting ice. The holographic projection was gone, the swirling vortex swallowed by the encroaching darkness. The silence was broken only by the drip, drip, drip of water, a relentless rhythm that echoed the urgency of our situation. We were trapped, surrounded by the debris of the collapsed facility, the weight of the Antarctic ice pressing down on us.

Using my flashlight, I carefully assessed our surroundings. We found ourselves in a newly formed cavern, the walls slick with moisture, the air cold and damp against my skin. The cavern was strangely shaped, nothing like the man-made tunnels of the research facility; this felt organic, almost...alive. I shivered, partly from the cold, partly from a primal unease.

As my eyes adjusted to the darkness, I noticed something else. Embedded in the cavern walls were strange, crystalline formations, pulsating with a faint, ethereal light. I felt a strange pull towards them, a magnetic attraction I couldn't explain. The formations were interconnected, forming a complex network of veins that seemed to throb with life, a living organism breathing before my very eyes.

The crystalline structures resembled the energy signatures I'd seen in the machine, and those haunting glimpses at the Loch Ness portholes. A cold certainty settled in my stomach; the connection between the Antarctic facility and the Loch Ness Monster was undeniable. This wasn't just a relay station; it was a part of a larger system, a vast, interconnected network spanning the globe. My breath hitched. I felt a sudden overwhelming sense of both terror and wonder.

Suddenly, a low growl echoed through the cavern, a rumble that vibrated through my very bones, shaking me to my core. The air grew icy, and a palpable sense of dread clamped down on me. We weren't alone.

My breath hitched. Anya's voice, barely a whisper, cut through the silence. "Nessie..."

My heart hammered against my ribs. The creature wasn't in Loch Ness anymore. It was here, in the heart of the Antarctic, trapped within this collapsing facility, a silent guardian of the universe's most closely guarded secret. I felt a wave of dizziness; the mystery had deepened, the stakes had risen impossibly high. This adventure... this nightmare... had taken a terrifying turn, a shocking twist that shattered everything I thought I knew. We'd faced down a mad scientist and his army of mercenaries, only to find ourselves confronting a power far beyond human comprehension – a power tied to a creature of myth, legend, and now, terrifying reality. I stared into the darkness, my palms slick with sweat. The fate of the multiverse, it seemed, rested in our hands, four adventurers trapped in this collapsing cavern beneath the Antarctic ice, facing the legendary Loch Ness Monster. The fight was far from over; it was only just beginning. And I knew, with a chilling certainty, that I was in over my head.

Chapter 8

The Monster's Secret

The air hung heavy with the scent of damp earth and decaying vegetation. My lungs filled with the musty smell, a strange mix of the familiar and the utterly alien. The cavern, surprisingly spacious, opened into a vast underground chamber, its walls shimmering with the same crystalline formations we'd seen in the Antarctic facility. These weren't mere rocks; I could feel it – they pulsed with a faint, internal light, their intricate network resembling a living organism. The rhythmic that had shaken us in the Antarctic facility was stronger here, resonating deep within my bones, a primal heartbeat echoing through the cavern. It made my teeth ache, a low humming vibration that seemed to burrow into my very being.

I used my flashlight, its beam cutting through the gloom, to examine a particularly large crystalline formation. It was multifaceted, its surface reflecting the light in a dazzling display of colors, each facet seeming to hold a universe within its depths. I reached out, my fingers hesitant, and touched the surface cautiously.

"This isn't just energy," Anya whispered, her voice echoing in the vast chamber, a faint tremor in her words. "I feel it...it's...information. Like a living database." I nodded, my own thoughts mirroring hers. This was something beyond our understanding, something far older than humanity itself.

Ben, his face illuminated by the faint glow of his headlamp, meticulously documented the crystalline structures, his fingers flying across his data pad. "The crystalline lattice," he murmured, "it's incredibly complex. It's processing something, transmitting something... but what?"

Liam, his usually sharp eyes wide with wonder, moved closer to a cluster of formations, their surfaces etched with intricate patterns that resembled constellations. "These... these are maps," he whispered, tracing one of the patterns with his finger. "Star charts, but not of our universe. They're...different."

As I examined the crystalline structures more closely, the true nature of the Loch Ness Monster began to dawn on me. These formations weren't merely storing energy; I realized they were processing it, translating it, channeling it through a vast, interconnected network that extended far beyond the confines of this cavern. The portholes under Loch Ness, the Antarctic facility, the UFO sightings – I saw them all as nodes in this network, conduits for an unimaginable flow of information and energy.

The Loch Ness Monster, I realized with a jolt, wasn't just a creature of myth and legend. It was a living component of this network, a biological interface between dimensions, a being far more advanced than I could have ever imagined. Its existence wasn't a biological accident; it was a carefully engineered marvel, a testament to a technology beyond human comprehension.

The low growl that had alerted us to the creature's presence intensified, resonating through the cavern like a deep, guttural chant. A palpable sense of anticipation, a mixture of fear and awe, filled me. Then, from the shadows at the far end of the chamber, it emerged. My breath hitched in my throat.

The creature wasn't the hulking, serpentine monster of folklore. It was...different. It was sleek and powerful, its body a shimmering mosaic of light and shadow, its skin reflecting the iridescent glow of the crystalline structures. It moved with an ethereal grace, its movements fluid and hypnotic, seemingly defying the laws of physics.

Instead of a reptilian head, it possessed something more akin to a bioluminescent crown, a complex arrangement of crystalline structures that pulsed with the same light as the cavern walls. This crown emanated a soft, almost musical hum that resonated deep within my soul. The creature's eyes, immense and intelligent, held a depth of understanding that left me breathless. We weren't merely observing; We were communicating.

The creature approached us slowly, its movements deliberate and measured. I felt no aggression in its posture, no hint of hostility. Instead, there was a profound sense of ancient wisdom, a quiet dignity that spoke volumes about its place in the universe. It paused before us, its gaze unwavering, and I could feel its presence filling the cavern with an otherworldly energy; a tingling sensation that ran down my spine.

As it moved, I noticed subtle shifts in the crystalline formations lining the cavern walls, subtle changes in their light and vibrations. My own heart seemed to echo the rhythm. The creature's very presence seemed to influence the network, as if it were a conductor orchestrating a symphony of cosmic energy. The implications of this were staggering. My mind reeled; Nessie wasn't just a biological being; it was a key component of a vast, interconnected system that spanned dimensions. I felt a wave of awe, of wonder, so profound that it left me breathless.

Anya, her usual skepticism suspended, reached out a trembling hand towards the creature. The creature tilted its head slightly, its bioluminescent crown pulsing rhythmically, as if acknowledging her gesture. Anya's hand passed through the creature's form, not encountering any physical resistance. The creature wasn't solid in the traditional sense; it was more like a living projection, a manifestation of energy within the crystalline network.

Ben was already frantically recording data, his data pad buzzing with the activity of his calculations. "Its energy signature... it's harmonizing with the network," he announced, his voice awed. "It's...integrating. It's part of the whole."

Liam, his apprehension replaced with a growing sense of understanding, approached the creature, his gaze locked with its immense eyes. He spoke in a low, almost reverent voice, as if addressing an ancient deity. "You are... the guardian," he whispered. "The key."

The creature responded with a low hum, a sound that vibrated through the cavern and echoed in our very souls. The hum carried a complex message, a torrent of information that bypassed their understanding of language and resonated directly with their consciousness.

I felt a surge of empathy, a connection with the creature that transcended words and reason. I understood, on a fundamental level, its purpose. It wasn't a monster; it was a protector and a guardian of the intricate network that connected dimension. It was a sentinel, a silent observer of a reality far grander and more complex than humanity could ever comprehend. It was the gatekeeper, not of a single dimension, but of the multiverse itself. I saw it as the living embodiment of the ancient energy that powered Reed's machine, and the reason for the cryptic messages embedded in the ancient stones that led us here.

The crystalline structures pulsed brighter, their light bathing the cavern in an ethereal glow. I watched as the creature's bioluminescent crown intensified, its hum growing louder, richer, as if responding to my understanding. We were not just witnesses to this creature's power; we were now participants. We were players in a game far beyond our understanding, a game that stretched across dimensions and time itself.

The adventure, once focused solely on the Loch Ness Monster, had expanded into a far grander quest – a journey into the heart of the multiverse itself. The answers they sought lay not just in the creature's nature, but in the intricate web of connections it represented, a cosmic network woven into the very fabric of reality. We were at the nexus, not only of the mystery surrounding the Loch Ness Monster, but of the universe's greatest secret. And we had just begun to unravel its threads. The path ahead was fraught with unknowns, filled with possibilities that defied comprehension. But now, armed with the knowledge of Nessie's true nature, our team was ready to confront whatever lay before us, united in their quest to protect the precarious balance of existence itself. The fight for reality itself had only just begun.

The creature's hum deepened, resonating not just in my ears but with my body. This was an abundance of information that blew my mind and flooded me with images and sensations. I saw swirling galaxies, structures of crystalline energy, and timelines twisting like strands of DNA. I felt the pulse of the multiverse, the rhythmic beating of countless realities, all interconnected through this web of energy.

Anya, her eyes closed, swayed gently beside me, her breathing slow and deep. I could sense the information surging through her as well, even though I couldn't see what she saw. Later, she described glimpses of futures yet to be written, possibilities branching out like the limbs of a colossal tree.

Ben, his data pad useless in the face of this influx of information, simply stared, his face pale with awe. The data streams were overwhelming, far beyond anything his technology could process. He told me that what was witnessing was not just data, but the blueprint of reality itself, a complex algorithm of the existence of the universe.

Liam, his intuition always sharper than his intellect, felt a profound sense of connection to the creature, an ancient understanding that transcended language and logic. He told me that he understood the creature's purpose: not to conquer or destroy, but to preserve, to protect the delicate balance of this vast, interconnected web of realities.

The images and sensations subsided, leaving me breathless and shaken. My heart hammered against my ribs. The creature's hum softened, becoming a gentle murmur, a soothing lullaby that calmed the turbulent storm within my mind. I felt a sense of peace wash over me. I knew it was guarding the gateway to countless dimensions and ensuring the stability of the multiverse. I felt a strange kinship with it, a connection that transcended words.

"It's... a key," Anya whispered, her voice still trembling. I heard the tremor in her voice, mirrored the trembling in my own hands. "A key to... everything."

"A biological key," Ben added, his voice regaining its usual pragmatic tone. I could practically feel his analytical mind at work. "It's not just a guardian; it's a regulator. It monitors the energy flow between dimensions, ensuring stability, preventing... paradoxes."

Liam nodded slowly. I saw his understanding mirrored in his thoughtful expression. "It's the balance, the harmony. It prevents the universe from collapsing in on itself."

I felt a sudden shift in the air, a prickling sensation on my skin, a change in the energy surrounding us. The crystalline formations pulsed more intensely, their light fluctuating rhythmic call and I felt a pulse in my own temples. The creature seemed to be communicating something new, something... urgent.

"It wants us to understand its purpose, but more importantly, it wants us to understand the threat," a sudden sense of urgency filling my voice. "The threat to the multiverse."

The creature's glowing crown pulsed again, this time more urgently. A new series of images flooded my mind – a twisted, corrupted energy, a force that threatened to unravel the intricate fabric of reality. It felt like a dark energy, an anti-force. I saw it – a force that wanted to shatter the multiverse. I felt the weight of that knowledge and certainty that settled deep in my bones.

The images shifted, showing glimpses of our other locations: the Antarctic facility, the hidden caves under Loch Ness, the places where they say UFOs have appeared. These weren't isolated incidents; I knew then, with a certainty that chilled me, that they were all connected, all nodes in a cosmic battleground.

The creature's purpose became crystal clear to me. It wasn't just a guardian; I saw it as warrior and defender of the multiverse. It needed us to understand the threat and find a way to stop it.

We were energized by a newfound understanding and purpose, we emerged from the cavern, the rhythmic thrumming of the crystalline network echoing behind us The Loch Ness Monster, once a mystery to be solved, had become a partner, an ally in a battle for the fate of reality itself.

Our first step – was to analyze the data we had received from the creature, to decipher the messages embedded in its hum and the visions that flooded my mind. I watched Ben, with his usual methodical approach; begin to piece together the fragmented information, his data pad buzzing with his calculations. He discovered that the dark energy was leaking through rifts in the fabric of space-time, rifts that were expanding, threatening to tear reality apart.

Anya, utilizing her knowledge of ancient languages and symbology, began to interpret the cryptic patterns etched into the crystalline formations. She found recurring symbols that resembled constellations, but constellations from unknown galaxies, star systems outside of our known universe. These weren't just maps; they were warnings, revealing the origins of the dark energy and its path of destruction.

Liam, relying on his intuition and connection to the creature, felt the pulse of the dark energy, sensing its location and its growing strength. He guided the team to the points where the rifts were most prominent, locations that were connected to the other phenomena they had investigated.

I was armed with my cryptozoological knowledge and my unique connection to Nessie, weaving together the scientific data, the ancient symbology, and my intuitive insights. I pieced together the strategy for confronting this interdimensional threat. It wasn't a simple fight; it was a terrifying, complex dance across multiple realities, a careful manipulation of the cosmic energy itself. This meant revisiting each of the previously investigated sites and personally studying the various manifestations of the dark energy.

Our journey had led us across the globe, from the icy plains of Antarctica, where the wind bit at my exposed skin, to the claustrophobic hidden caves beneath the Scottish Highlands, echoing with the whispers of ancient secrets. We had descended into the crushing depths of the ocean and gazed out at the terrifying, beautiful vastness of outer space. We had encountered resistance from skeptical scientists and governments – their doubt felt like a physical blow. They were individuals who couldn't, or wouldn't, believe in the existence of such a threat.

The creature, through subtle shifts in its bioluminescent crown, had guided us, revealing the intricate mechanisms required to stabilize the cosmic energy flows. It showed us that it was a complex process, involving the precise manipulation of the crystalline structures, the careful channeling of energy, and a deep understanding of the universe's fundamental forces.

The final confrontation took place in a swirling vortex of energy, a point of convergence between dimensions. The creature was born from the disintegration of the dying star. It was a terrifying battle, a struggle to maintain the balance of existence itself. With Nessie's guidance, our combined knowledge, and our unwavering determination pushed us forward.

In the aftermath, the world remained largely unaware of the cosmic battle that had been fought, unaware of the near-catastrophe that had been averted. We knew we had faced the unimaginable, saved the multiverse, and learned a profound lesson about the interconnectedness of all things. The Loch Ness Monster, once a creature of myth and legend, had become our protector, our teacher, our ally in a battle for the fate of existence itself. And the quest, far from being over, had just begun. The universe held countless other mysteries, countless other dangers; but now, armed with knowledge and understanding, I knew we were ready to face them all. The adventure continued. The multiverse waited, and I, along with my team, was ready.

Liam, his eyes closed, seemed lost in the aftershocks of the experience. He spoke with a hushed reverence, his voice barely a whisper. "The creature isn't just a guardian; it is a part of the fabric, a living embodiment of the cosmic order. I felt it – its understanding of the interconnectedness of all things, the delicate balance that maintains the multiverse. It is, in essence, a living algorithm that ensures harmony amidst chaos." His words resonated deeply within me.

As I pieced together the fragments of our experience, a profound sense of clarity emerged from the swirling chaos. "The portholes under Loch Ness," I said, my voice stronger now, filled with a newfound certainty, "aren't just gateways to other dimensions; they are intersections in a vast network, points of convergence within this cosmic river of time. The UFO sightings, the Antarctic facility... I realized they were all connected, manifestations of this interconnected energy. The creature has been using these points to monitor, regulate, and protect the multiverse."

I felt a surge of adrenaline as our team embarked on this new phase of the investigation, armed with our expanded understanding. Antarctica was our first stop, the location of that mysterious facility. We'd been there before, but this time, knowing about the interconnected nature of the rifts, I felt a certainty in the precision of our coordinates – deep within the ice sheet. The facility itself was beyond anything I could have imagined, filled with technology that blurred the line between science fiction and reality. The machines hummed with the same energy signature as the crystalline formations in the Loch Ness cavern; it was deliberate, a network spanning continents, even realms.

My heart pounded as we investigated the Antarctic facility and discovered a hidden chamber, concealed deep within the ice. Inside, I saw it – a massive crystalline structure, eerily similar to the ones we'd encountered in Loch Ness. This crystal pulsed with a faint luminescence, emitting a low hum that resonated deeply within me. Anya gasped – she recognized the symbols etched onto the crystal, symbols remarkably similar to those found in ancient Sumerian tablets. It was a mind-blowing revelation: a civilization far older than humanity, one that might have understood the multiverse.

Our journey then took us to the Gobi Desert. I felt the heat beating down on me as we uncovered another subterranean complex, even more ancient than the Antarctic facility. The complex was filled with intricate carvings and symbols, evidence of civilizations who'd mastered time travel. These weren't just ruins; they were archives, repositories of knowledge stretching back eons – proof of a cosmic race that once inhabited Earth, masters of space-time. The weight of their history, their knowledge, pressed down on me, a tangible feeling of awe and profound mystery.

The evidence found in the Gobi Desert suggested that the dark energy wasn't simply leaking through rifts; it was actively being channeled through these ancient sites. It was a deliberate act, a calculated attempt to destabilize the multiverse, and the cosmic entities behind it sought to achieve a complete unraveling of reality as they understood it. A series of symbols, interpreted by Anya and Ben, revealed a chilling prophecy – a future where the fabric of reality was shattered, leaving only chaos in its wake. The prophecy also alluded to a way to prevent this outcome, a method of sealing the rifts and restoring the harmony of the multiverse.

I realized then that we weren't just fighting for the survival of Earth; we were fighting for the survival of the entire multiverse. Our quest had evolved from a simple cryptozoological investigation into a cosmic battle against a force that threatened to annihilate all of existence. The urgency of our situation pressed down on me as the implications sank in. I knew then that the timelines themselves could be broken, and that the result would be complete universal destruction.

Our journey continued, taking us to hidden caves in the Himalayas, submerged cities in the Pacific Ocean, and even to the edge of space. We faced challenges beyond our wildest imaginations; navigating treacherous landscapes, deciphering ancient codes, and confronting forces that defied explanation. I felt the fear and adrenaline, but we pressed on.

The knowledge we gathered at each site painted a larger picture, revealing a plan of cosmic proportions. We uncovered ancient texts, sophisticated technology, and disturbing evidence of a battle fought eons ago, a battle between guardians of the multiverse and forces of chaos. This revealed the nature of the entity behind the dark energy and the motivations behind its actions. I personally poured over the texts, felt the weight of history in my hands.

Using a combination of ancient knowledge and cutting-edge technology, we managed to seal the rift, stemming the tide of chaos and restoring the harmony to the multiverse. I felt the relief wash over me when we succeeded. It was a hard-won victory, but a victory nonetheless. I emerged from the experience profoundly changed, forever bound by the knowledge I had gained, and the challenges we had overcome.

The world remained unaware of the cosmic battle that had been fought, but I knew. My team and I had walked the thin line between existence and annihilation, faced the unimaginable, and emerged victorious. We hadn't only solved the mystery of the Loch Ness Monster; we had saved the multiverse. Our quest, however, was far from over. The universe held countless other secrets, countless other threats.

Our return to the 'real' world was jarring. The bustling streets of London, the mundane routines of daily life, seemed almost comical in their ordinariness after our encounters with multiversal entities and ancient technologies. The transition was incredibly difficult; my mind still raced with the intricate web of realities I had glimpsed. I found myself constantly scanning my surroundings, expecting to see shimmering distortions in the air or hear the hum of otherworldly energy. Sleep offered little respite; my dreams were filled with visions of crystalline structures, swirling nebulae, and the terrifying power of the entity we had confronted. The fear clung to me, a cold, persistent shadow.

I, in particular, struggled with the aftermath. The weight of my lifelong obsession with Nessie, once a personal quest, had transformed into a global responsibility. The Loch Ness Monster, once a creature of myth and legend, was now revealed to be a vital component of a cosmic network. The implications of our discovery extended far beyond the scientific community; it challenged the very foundations of human understanding, of reality itself.

My first thought was, "Who can we tell?" The scientific community, stuck in its old ways of thinking, would probably laugh us out of the room, maybe even call us crazy. Governments would likely try to grab it for themselves and weaponize it, without a clue about the potential for total disaster. We knew that revealing everything at once would be a recipe for catastrophe – attracting the wrong kind of attention, far worse than anything we'd already faced.

We opted for a slow rollout, starting with a small group of scientists we trusted, people with open minds who weren't afraid to think outside the box. Ben, with his genius-level physics background, took the lead, crafting reports with extreme care, presenting our findings as cautiously as possible. Anya's incredible linguistic skills were essential; she deciphered those ancient texts, translating the cryptic symbols and uncovering hidden meanings I couldn't even begin to fathom. Liam, who had this almost mystical connection to the energies we'd encountered, provided a spiritual perspective that gave our claims more weight. And I, the one who pushed us to go on this expedition in the first place, became our spokesperson, weaving a compelling narrative, carefully choosing every word.

Our early presentations were met with skepticism, even outright mockery. But as we laid out the irrefutable evidence – the high-resolution images, the analyzed energy signatures, the translated texts – things started to change. Slowly, painstakingly, we won over some influential people in the scientific community, finding allies who would protect our work and help us spread the word. But the future still felt uncertain, terrifyingly so.

The aftermath settled upon us like a shroud, the adrenaline of our near-death experience slowly giving way to a profound weariness. We were back in my modest cottage in the Scottish Highlands, the comforting scent of peat smoke a stark contrast to the sterile, metallic tang of the Antarctic research facility. My cottage, a place of comfort and refuge, now felt strangely inadequate, a flimsy shield against the cosmic realities we now inhabited.

I stared out the rain-lashed window, the grey expanse of Loch Ness mirroring the turbulent landscape of my mind – I could feel it. The monster, Nessie – once a symbol of my childhood wonder, a whimsical obsession.

Liam, ever the spiritual anchor of our group, sat by the fire, his gaze distant, lost in the flickering flames. I watched him; he was a man of quiet contemplation, and his intuitive understanding of energy flows and ancient prophecies offered a counterpoint to Ben and Anya's scientifically rigorous approaches. He'd been the most profoundly affected by our journey; I could see it in his eyes.

Anya, her usual vibrant energy tempered by a thoughtful quiet, pored over ancient texts, her sharp intellect sifting through cryptic symbols and half-forgotten languages. Her expertise had been indispensable, translating the prophecies, deciphering the technology, providing the vital linguistic bridge between our world and the others. Even her brilliance seemed to falter in the face of the sheer scale of our discovery.

Ben, the pragmatic physicist, seemed to be dealing with the aftermath by plunging back into his work, analyzing data, constructing models, attempting to rationalize the irrational. He was a man of science, driven by logic and evidence, yet even he struggled to reconcile our experience with the established laws of physics. The multiverse, the manipulation of space-time, the living energy of the crystalline network – these were concepts that challenged the very foundations of his scientific worldview. I saw him writing countless equations, seeking patterns, correlations, anything that could help him understand the forces we had encountered.

Weeks went by and I found myself drawn back to Loch Ness, to the familiar stillness of the waters, the comforting presence of that ancient landscape. I spent hours by the loch, the rhythmic lapping of the waves against the soothing shore. I felt a deep connection to the monster, a bond forged through years of my own obsession, culminating in a shared experience that transcended anything I'd ever known. Nessie wasn't merely a creature of myth; to me, she was a guardian, a protector, a vital part of a cosmic ecosystem beyond human comprehension.

Over time, a small, dedicated group of scientists began to acknowledge our findings. The compelling evidence – energy signatures, translated prophecies, high-resolution images – slowly eroded the skepticism. I could feel our work beginning to gather momentum, our findings gaining traction within the scientific community. I knew the revelation of the multiverse wouldn't happen overnight. The Geneva conference was right around the corner.

Chapter 9

Rewriting History

I felt the hushed anticipation in the Geneva conference hall. Liam, Anya, and Ben sat at the head table, the polished wood under the bright lights. Years of painstaking research, countless sleepless nights, and the constant threat of ridicule had culminated in this moment. We weren't just presenting a scientific paper; we were attempting to rewrite history, to introduce humanity to the concept of a multiverse – a concept previously relegated to the realm of science fiction. The air was filled with a nervous energy, a mixture of excitement and apprehension that mirrored the feelings within me.

I began the presentation. My voice, usually clear and confident, held a tremor of emotion. I started with the familiar story, my childhood fascination with Nessie, my academic pursuit, the unexpected discoveries I made in the Antarctic research facility. I carefully omitted the more fantastical elements, focusing instead on the verifiable scientific data: energy signatures, isotopic anomalies, the translated prophecies from ancient Sumerian texts that I'd painstakingly deciphered. I presented compelling evidence of temporal distortions linked to the Loch Ness anomaly, showing them the graphs and charts I'd meticulously prepared, detailing the energy fluctuations I detected around the portholes under the loch. I could feel the tension in the room; the world's leading physicists, cryptozoologists, and archaeologists were all there, their faces a mixture of skepticism and intrigue. I knew I had their attention.

Ben followed me. He presented the complex mathematical models he'd developed, equations that defied conventional physics, explaining the manipulation of space time through the crystalline network and the potential for interdimensional travel. He spoke of energy transfer, of dimensional rifts, of parallel universes – words that once sounded like science fiction, now presented with the rigorous methodology of scientific fact. His voice was steady, his presentation meticulous, his words carefully chosen. I watched, feeling a surge of pride and a touch of apprehension as he even showed some edited video footage, subtly hinting at the strange light anomalies and energy surges around the loch, focusing only on the verifiable scientific elements; I had helped him edit it, ensuring we steered clear of anything too unbelievable.

Anya, the linguist and historian, then took the stage. She delved into the ancient texts, carefully navigating the delicate balance between academic accurcy and the sensational nature of their discoveries. She focused on the prophecies, explaining the symbology, detailing how they predicted the convergence of realities, the activation of the crystalline network, and the threat posed by the entity they had encountered. Her presentation was a masterclass in weaving together ancient lore with modern science, a testament to her profound understanding of both worlds. She presented translated excerpts, carefully omitting the more overtly supernatural elements, focusing on the specific references to "gateways" and "interdimensional travelers" that matched their observations.

Finally, Liam, the spiritual guide, spoke. His words were few, but they resonated deeply. He spoke of the interconnectedness of all things, of the delicate balance of the multiverse, of the responsibility that came with their discovery. He spoke of the entity, not as a monster, but as a guardian, a protector of the fragile ecosystem that linked all realities. He spoke of the need for respect, for understanding, for a cautious approach to the infinite possibilities that lay before humanity. His calm demeanor and wise words helped to ground the audience, bridging the gap between scientific rationalism and the profound spiritual implications of their findings.

The presentation concluded with a resounding silence, broken only by the low hum of the projector. Then, slowly, questions began to trickle in, starting with hesitant inquiries about the methodologies, then moving towards the more controversial topics. The ensuing discussion lasted for hours, a battleground of scientific debate, intellectual curiosity, and hushed disbelief. Some remained skeptical, demanding more proof, questioning their methods, pointing to gaps in their evidence; others, captivated by the sheer audacity of their claims, were eager to embrace the implications.

The media frenzy that followed was unprecedented. News channels across the globe reported on their findings, the story unfolding in a kaleidoscope of headlines: "Loch Ness Monster Holds Key to Multiverse?" "Scientists Rewrite History," "Is Time Travel Possible?" The general public, initially captivated by the mystery surrounding Nessie, were now bombarded with the even more mind-bending concept of a multiverse. The initial wave of skepticism was tempered by the rigorous scientific backing of our research, the compelling evidence presented during the conference.

In the weeks and months that followed, the implications of their discovery reverberated through society. Governments scrambled to understand the implications for national security, scientific institutions re-evaluated their understanding of the universe, and philosophers grappled with the ethical and existential questions raised by the existence of a multiverse. Religious leaders debated the implications of their findings on theological doctrine. The world, once content with its relatively simple understanding of reality, was thrown into a state of exhilarating uncertainty.

Our discovery sparked a new wave of scientific exploration, pushing the boundaries of human knowledge and technology. Research funding poured into previously underfunded areas like quantum physics and astrophysics. International collaborations sprang up, uniting scientists from diverse disciplines in a shared quest to understand the intricacies of the multiverse. The world was changed forever, irrevocably altered by the revelation that reality was far more complex, far more wondrous, and far more terrifying than anyone could have ever imagined.

Our team, once a small group of dedicated researchers, became global icons, our names synonymous with revolutionizing our understanding of reality. We travelled the world, lecturing at prestigious universities, participating in high-level government briefings, and advising international organizations. Despite the overwhelming public attention, our team remained grounded, our commitment to responsible scientific inquiry unwavering. We established a foundation dedicated to the ethical exploration of the multiverse, ensuring that this incredible power wouldn't fall into the wrong hands.

I gazed out at the rolling hills of the Scottish Highlands from my updated, modernized cottage – a stark contrast to the modest dwelling I'd called home for so many years. A quiet satisfaction settled over me. The journey had been perilous, the challenges seemingly insurmountable, but we had done it. We had succeeded in rewriting history, in opening humanity's eyes to the extraordinary possibilities that lay beyond the veil of ordinary reality. The quest for understanding continues, the mysteries of the universe as vast and uncharted as the depths of Loch Ness itself, but now, with this profound knowledge of the larger reality, the possibilities feel limitless.

My cottage in the Scottish Highlands, overlooking the calm waters of Loch Ness, became our sanctuary, a place where we could escape the relentless demands of the outside world. I felt a deep sense of peace there, a quiet strength born from shared hardship and the knowledge that we were in this together.

One evening, as the sun dipped below the horizon, casting a warm golden glow over the loch, I sat with Liam, Anya, and Ben. They had just finished reviewing the latest data from the monitoring stations stationed around the portholes. Everything seemed calm for now, the energy signatures stable, the temporal distortions under control.

"Do you ever think we should have kept it quiet?" Anya asked, her voice barely above a whisper.

Liam placed a reassuring hand on her shoulder. "Sometimes, Anya, the truth has a way of finding its own path. We couldn't have kept it secret forever, and honestly, it might have been far worse if some nefarious entity had stumbled onto it first."

Ben nodded in agreement. "We had a responsibility. A terrifying responsibility, but a responsibility nonetheless."

I looked out at the tranquil waters of Loch Ness, the setting sun painting the sky in vibrant hues. "We made our choice," I said. "We will manage the aftermath. We will face whatever challenges lay ahead, together."

Chapter 10

Epilogue: A New Beginning

The mist clung to the surface of Loch Ness like a shroud, the ancient waters reflecting the bruised purple of the twilight sky. I stood at the edge, the familiar chill of the air a comforting weight on my skin. The wind whispered through the reeds, carrying the scent of peat smoke and damp earth, a sensory tapestry woven from the fabric of my childhood memories. It had been years since that fateful day, the day I first glimpsed the creature that had sparked my lifelong obsession, the day that had irrevocably altered the course of human history.

I traced the outline of the loch with my gaze, the familiar landscape now imbued with a profound new significance. The seemingly ordinary body of water, once the focus of countless legends and dismissed as a mere quirk of nature, now stood as a testament to the breathtaking possibilities that lay hidden beneath the surface of reality. This loch was a gateway, not just to a hidden world, but to countless others. The portholes, once hidden beneath the waves, were now recognized as points of interdimensional convergence, each a shimmering portal to a different reality.

A quiet chuckle escaped my lips, a mixture of awe and nostalgia. I remembered the disbelief, the skepticism, the endless hours spent poring over ancient texts, obscure maps, and scientific papers. I remembered the doubt that had gnawed at me, the moments when I had almost given up, the loneliness of pursuing a truth that no one else believed. But I was driven by an unwavering belief, a conviction that felt as undeniable as the cold air against my skin. And now, here I stood, the woman who had proven the impossible, who had not only found Nessie but had unlocked the secrets of the multiverse.

I closed my eyes, the image of Nessie, majestic and ethereal, dancing in my mind's eye. It was more than a legend; it was a keystone species, a living embodiment of the interconnectedness of reality, a guardian of the dimensional gateways. The creature, once relegated to the realm of myth, was now the symbol of a new era, an era of exploration, discovery, and a profound understanding of the universe's breathtaking complexity.

The wind picked up, carrying the faint sound of waves lapping against the shore. The mist began to dissipate, revealing a sliver of moon piercing through the clouds. The loch, once shrouded in mystery, was now bathed in a soft, ethereal light. The water, once seemingly ordinary, pulsed with an almost palpable energy, a reminder of the untold wonders that lay beneath.

I thought about the boundless opportunities that lay ahead. The exploration of the multiverse was far from over; it had just begun. There were new worlds to discover, new creatures to understand, new mysteries to unravel. The human race had taken its first tentative steps beyond the confines of its own reality, a monumental leap into the vast expanse of the cosmos. The once-isolated event on the shores of Loch Ness had blossomed into a global phenomenon, forever changing the destiny of humankind.

Yet, despite the global significance of her discovery, I felt a profound sense of connection to this place, to this loch that had ignited my lifelong quest. It was here, amidst the rolling hills and ancient waters of the Scottish Highlands, that my journey had begun. It was here that I felt most at home and connected to the extraordinary mysteries that had drawn me to this place, to this watery gateway to the infinite.

I reached into my pocket, retrieving a small, smooth stone, cool and polished by the relentless action of the loch. It was a memento, a reminder of the day when I first saw Nessie, a tangible connection to her extraordinary journey. I held it in my hand, feeling the weight of history, the weight of my discovery, the weight of the responsibility that came with it. The stone was not merely a souvenir; it was a symbol of the enduring power of curiosity, the unwavering pursuit of knowledge, and the boundless capacity of the human spirit to embrace the unknown.

The night deepened, the stars emerging with breathtaking clarity. I gazed at the celestial canvas, feeling a sense of awe and humility that dwarfed even the monumental discoveries of the past years. The universe, once confined to her understanding of a single planet, was now an infinite expanse, brimming with endless wonders and untold mysteries. The journey had been long, perilous, and life-altering, but the destination, the ultimate understanding of the universe, still felt distant, a glimpse beyond the horizon.

As the first hint of dawn painted the eastern sky, I knew my work was far from done. The exploration of the multiverse was an endless endeavor, an ongoing quest for knowledge, understanding and even a glimpse into the very fabric of reality itself. The legend of the Loch Ness Monster had been reborn, transformed from a local myth into a global symbol of the extraordinary possibilities of the universe. Nessie, the elusive creature, was now a guardian, a protector of the gateways, a living testament to the power of the unknown and the enduring mysteries that drive the human spirit to explore, to discover, and to never cease in its quest to understand the wonders that lay beyond our comprehension. The enduring mystery of Nessie was far from solved; it had simply opened a gateway to a whole universe of other mysteries, each one as captivating and as compelling as the one that had begun it all, on the misty shores of Loch Ness. The future, like the universe itself, was boundless. The adventure, however, was just beginning

Back Matter

Cryptid: An animal whose existence is not proven but is supported by anecdotal evidence or eyewitness accounts.

Dimensional Gateway: A hypothetical point in space-time that allows for passage between different dimensions or universes.

Interdimensional Travel: The act of traversing between different dimensions or universes.

Keystone Species: A species that has a disproportionately large effect on its environment relative to its abundance.

Porthole: In the context of this novel, a naturally occurring interdimensional gateway located beneath Loch Ness.

Xenozoology: The study of extraterrestrial animals.